Y0-BWS-235

*Aaron had been bitten by an
adventure bug*

Abby's normally levelheaded, conservative boss was
picturing himself as something between Mark Twain
and Indiana Jones. It was her duty to remain the
voice of reason.

"You're not thinking this through. What are the
girls going to do while you're preoccupied with
steering this houseboat?"

"Why, they'll be wide-eyed with wonder, taking in
all the scenery."

"I mean, twenty minutes after you take off."

Aaron's lips flattened into a grim line, creating an
expression Abby had seen too often to find
intimidating. "Abby, give me some credit. I've
thought about it myself, and I think I've come up
with a great solution."

"Aaron, I don't think your housekeeper sees a
houseboat ride up the Mississippi as a negotiable
item."

"I wasn't planning to take my housekeeper," Aaron
replied with a shrug. "I'm taking *you*."

Dear Reader,

April . . . the month of showers. Hopefully you'll
have a bridal or baby shower in store for you or a
loved one this month. But if it's only the rainy-day
variety coming your way, don't get the blues, get a
Silhouette Romance novel and sneak back to bed for
a few hours of delightful romantic fantasy!

Silhouette Romance novels always reflect the magic
of love in compelling stories that will make you
laugh and cry. And this month is no exception. Our
heroines find happiness with the heroes of their
dreams—from the boy next door to the handsome,
mysterious stranger. We guarantee their heartwarming
stories will move you time and time again.

April continues our WRITTEN IN THE STARS
series. Each month in 1992 we're proud to present a
book that focuses on the hero and his astrological
sign. This month we're featuring the assertive Aries
man in Carla Cassidy's warm and wonderful
Whatever Alex Wants . . . .

In the months to come, watch for Silhouette
Romance novels by your all-time favorites, including
Diana Palmer, Suzanne Carey, Annette Broadrick,
Brittany Young and many, many more. The
Silhouette Romance authors and editors love to hear
from readers, and we'd love to hear from *you*.

Happy reading!

Valerie Susan Hayward
Senior Editor

HELEN R. MYERS

Three Little Chaperones

Silhouette Romance

Published by Silhouette Books New York

America's Publisher of Contemporary Romance

SILHOUETTE BOOKS
300 E. 42nd St., New York, N.Y. 10017

THREE LITTLE CHAPERONES

Copyright © 1992 by Helen R. Myers

ISBN: 0-373-08861-2

First Silhouette Books printing April 1992

All the characters in this book have no existence outside the
imagination of the author and have no relation whatsoever to
anyone bearing the same name or names. They are not even
distantly inspired by any individual known or unknown to the
author, and all incidents are pure invention.

®: Trademark used under license and registered in the United
States Patent and Trademark Office and in other countries.

Printed in the U.S.A.

Books by Helen R. Myers

Silhouette Romance

Donovan's Mermaid #557
Someone to Watch Over Me #643
Confidentially Yours #677
Invitation to a Wedding #737
A Fine Arrangement #776
Through My Eyes #814
Three Little Chaperones #861

Silhouette Desire

Partners for Life #370
Smooth Operator #454
That Fontaine Woman! #471
The Pirate O'Keefe #506
Kiss Me Kate #570
After You #599
When Gabriel Called #650

HELEN R. MYERS

satisfies her preference for a reclusive life-style by living deep in the piney woods of East Texas with her husband, Robert, and—because they were there first—the various species of four-legged and winged creatures that wander throughout their ranch. To write has been her lifelong dream, and to bring a slightly different flavor to each book is an ongoing ambition.

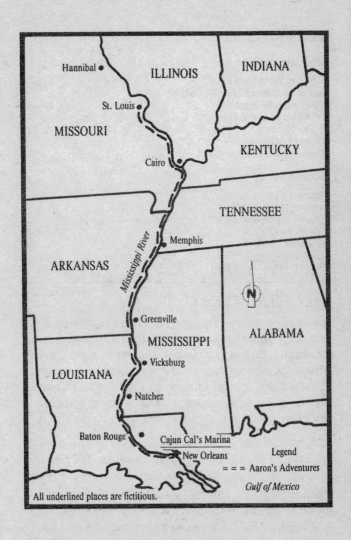

Hannibal • ILLINOIS   INDIANA

St. Louis •

MISSOURI

                    KENTUCKY

        Cairo •

                TENNESSEE

ARKANSAS   Mississippi River   • Memphis

                                N

            • Greenville

        MISSISSIPPI   ALABAMA

            • Vicksburg

LOUISIANA

            • Natchez

Baton Rouge •   Cajun Cal's Marina   Legend
                New Orleans   = = = Aaron's Adventures

All underlined places are fictitious.   Gulf of Mexico

Chapter One

"You're late."

Judge Aaron Mathias Marshall slumped against the closed door of his private chambers and checked his watch; after all, he decided, there was no point in wasting a perfectly good glare on Abby, since she had delivered her dubious greeting without bothering to look up from her desk. *Good grief.* He blinked at the gold-encircled analog display. How could it be only 9:17 when he was already too drained to count to ten? Never would he have believed it, but the children had only been with him four—no, three days—and they had already managed to do what D.A. Syd Wendell's assistants had been trying, albeit unsuccessfully, to accomplish for nearly five years. Somehow, they'd managed to take him, a reputedly intelligent, mature man of forty-two and push him to the edge of sanity.

Children? Hell. His nieces were three midget fiends.

"I had Delores reschedule your nine o'clock appointment to Thursday, and she's phoned down to the central jurors' room to push back your first case from nine-thirty to... Oh, my," Abigail Gordon mouthed, having finally glanced up from her work. "What did they do this time?"

As much as he normally valued his assistant's intuitive talents, her conclusion that he'd been on the losing end of yet another skirmish in the battle of wills with his pubescent houseguests added insult to injury. "What makes you think my darling charges have anything to do with my appearance?" he countered, summoning the last dredges of his aplomb. "Isn't it conceivable that I've just been mugged down in the parking garage?"

From behind tortoise-framed reading glasses, Abby's indigo blue eyes took on a suspicious twinkle. "Would you like me to call security and warn them to be on the lookout for a perpetrator who has peanut butter and jelly on his—or was it *her*—fingers?"

There were times, Aaron thought as he eyed the incontrovertible smear across what had been his freshly laundered white shirt, when it didn't even pay to crawl out of bed in the mornings. Without dignifying Abby's question with an answer, he tossed his jacket and briefcase onto the nearest chair and cut a straight course for the coffeemaker in the narrow utility room separating her office from his.

He no longer cared that during his previous physical his doctor had lectured about his excessive intake of caffeine; he poured a full dose of the aromatic brew into the hand-painted mug his secretary had given him last Christmas. Delores was a good soul, he thought, returning to Abby's office. Delores deserved a raise. Abby, he was beginning to suspect, no doubt had allied herself with his nieces and they were jointly plotting to drive him out of what was left of his mind.

He took a cautious sip and sighed with a mixture of relief and wariness. "I keep telling myself this isn't happening. I think maybe I indulged in one martini too many at Judge Underwood's last party... that it's really only May and my alarm is going to go off any second and I'll open my eyes to discover it's all been a bad dream ... that it isn't July and I don't really have three—three *persons* at my house who are, even as we speak, dismantling it, as though it's an extension of the Berlin Wall."

"You're the one who invited them."

Did he need the reminder? Aaron pinched the bridge of his nose, regret turning to guilt, and sarcasm giving way to fatigue. "Yes, I invited them, because Sean and Betsy were in dire need of this vacation. But I had no idea it was going to be like this. Abby, I'm not going to survive the week, let alone the entire month I promised they could have."

His suggested solution had seemed so logical two weeks ago, when Sean had phoned to discuss his dilemma. After nine years, his younger brother and sister-in-law's marriage was in danger of collapsing. Between the stress of Sean's demanding job as an editor with a Baltimore-based newsmagazine and Betsy's frustrations over having to sell out her interest in a budding catering business in order to take care of their three energetic daughters, the couple's personal relationship was practically nonexistent and their home was turning into a war zone.

In an everything-or-bust move, they had agreed to take a month off and focus on each other while there was still something left of their marriage to salvage. And that, Aaron thought dolefully, was where he'd made his own tactical error.

Except for Betsy's mother, he was the closest relation the girls had. With scatterbrained socialite Mavis off to South America for her fourth honeymoon, it had been clear to Aaron that he had been Sean and Betsy's only hope to take care of the girls—who, he understood, were all too aware of the tension between their parents. From the moment he'd picked them up at the airport, he had been trying to be stoic for them, fun and reassuring; but what he'd neglected to remember during all his planning was that, except for a few brief visits, he and the girls were virtual strangers. And, as of this morning, he'd come to the conclusion he had assumed responsibility for a task for which he was remarkably unqualified.

It wasn't that he didn't love the girls; they were part of Sean, so how could he not? He and his younger brother had always had a good relationship. They'd grown even closer after the death of their father, back when Aaron had been in law school and Sean in college. Nor were the girls impossible to handle...not always...at least not after he got them into bed for the night. He enjoyed tucking them in best, listening to their prayers, which were as heart-wrenching, with their childlike bluntness, as they could be amusing. They were so pink-skinned, drowsy-eyed and innocent-looking then, dressed in their ribbon-and-lace nighties. They made him think of Christmas-card angels.

Inevitably, however, dawn followed to clear his head of those musings, and the fiasco started all over again, just like a traveling three-ringed circus.

"I don't want that kind of cereal for breakfast."

"My shoe is missing a lace!"

"How do puppies get bored?" *Bored?* He was a bachelor; whatever had possessed him to think he could deal with such questions, let alone improve the language skills of three little girls?

Aaron didn't notice Abby rising from her desk or moving around him, until she took the mug out of his hand and replaced it with a glass of refrigerator-cooled vegetable juice. "You know I don't like this stuff," he protested, as she poured the coffee back into its pot.

"Force yourself to drink it, anyway. It has all kinds of vitamins and things that are good for you." She drew him to his own office. "Besides, knowing you, you skipped breakfast this morning."

"How could I think about eating? Mrs. Kaminski phoned to say she was going to be late. Someone had to get the kids fed. Do you have any idea what's involved in getting an eight-, seven- and five-year-old to ingest something edible? No two of them wanted the same thing. And even though she's the youngest, Mitch is the most independent. She insisted on preparing her own."

"Thus the peanut-butter-and-jelly swirl on your shirt?" Abby drawled, urging him into the black leather swivel chair behind his desk.

Once again Aaron woefully studied the smear just above his belt buckle. In all honesty, it looked better than some of the modern art displayed at those galleries Adrienne used to drag him through; however, being reminded of the woman he had recently stopped seeing didn't improve his mood.

When Adrienne Laurent had heard about his plans to be a temporary bachelor father, she'd kissed him goodbye—that is, after she stopped laughing. The chic divorcée had invited him to call her when he was alone again. Fat chance he would, though, Aaron assured himself with a scowl. As attractive and desirable as Adrienne was, he didn't need a woman in his life who was only willing to be around during the good times. No, better that he'd gleaned that tidbit of wisdom before things had grown more serious between them.

"She must have done this when she was trying to keep from falling off the kitchen bar stool," he told Abby. "No wonder her sisters were snickering when I left the house—and I guess by then Mrs. Kaminski was too upset with the state of the kitchen to pay attention to the way I looked." He set the juice glass on his blotter and reached for his tie. "Do I have any extra shirts here, or will I have to settle for rinsing this out in the sink?"

Instead of answering, Abby once again thrust the glass into his hand. Then she brushed the other one away from the tie, only to finish removing it herself. "I meant what I said, Aaron, drink your juice. With the schedule you have this morning, there won't be time to eat until around one this afternoon."

Now that he had her attention, he tried a glare. "Has anyone ever told you that you're one bossy woman?"

"Only you—" her tone, like her actions, were brisk with efficiency as next she dealt with the buttons on his shirt cuffs "—every time you get yourself into some mess that I have to resolve for you. Drink," she ordered, before he had a chance to protest. "I'll get a clean shirt out of the closet."

While he debated between laughing or firing her, Aaron eyed his assistant's trim back. As usual, she was clothed uninspiringly in a navy pin-striped jacket and skirt. The female rendition of a power suit.

After five years, Abby still treated him as if he were something between a slave driver and a bumbling adolescent; there rarely seemed to be any in-betweens with her. It was getting damned annoying considering it had been he who'd seen her potential soon after he'd hired her as his secretary; he who'd gone out of his way to be supportive after her personal tragedy; and he who had also encouraged her to finish her schooling. Then what about afterward, when he'd been so impressed with her accomplishment, he'd promoted her to be his assistant and researcher? With all that history between them, was it asking too much that she should credit him with having a modicum of common sense, let alone some ability to get through at least a portion of his life without her guidance?

Narrowing his eyes at the neat, pale blond bun at her nape, he wondered how she would like it if he started pointing out her shortcomings? For instance... well, there certainly was...Aaron frowned as he realized that nothing came to mind. Abby was the best secretary he'd ever had, and the only reason he had promoted her out of the position was because he knew she would be an even better assistant. She was intelligent, quick, intuitive and thorough; plus, she was as committed to her work as he was to his. They made an indomitable team; everyone said so. Truth be known—though he would consider eating liver before admitting it—he lived in constant dread that some other judge or high-rolling attorney would succeed in stealing her away from him. No, there was nothing about Abby he could criticize.

Except, he amended staring harder at that bun, the way she coiled her wonderful hair into a hideous knot. Now *that* was as criminal as her hiding her willowy figure beneath those severe business suits. How would she like it if he pointed out she was all but smothering the undeniably sexy woman she was? She'd been doing it for a while now, too. Heaven knows he was being the soul of discretion by not saying anything. He had kept silent because he'd been convinced it was a passing mood, part of the healing process, a way for her to deal with her depression over her miscarriage and the subsequent divorce from her ex-football-playing jock husband. Only four years was a damned sight long for a mood to linger. In fact, Abby was perfecting this image of hers into an art form.

She barely even wore any makeup these days, he noted as she drew the clean shirt from the closet. Not that she needed much; she had great bones and classical features. Even those reading glasses she hid behind couldn't conceal the truth, or the fact that her indigo blue eyes had alluring heavy lashes. Eyes so dark and mysterious were meant to be clouded with passion, not flashing with annoyance.

"Aaron, for heaven's sake, you have less than thirty minutes to review your notes for your first case. Don't just sit there."

Her rebuke—though spoken with more concern than agitation—snapped him out of his daydreaming. What had he been thinking? Passion! Maybe he was wise to worry about his sanity if he was starting to think about Abby that way. He took a gulp of the juice to help clear his head, only to grimace. "Blech." Even the offending drink was reduced to secondary importance, however, when Abby set the plastic-covered shirt on his desk and leaned over to start unbuttoning his soiled one. "I'm not completely helpless, you know."

"No, of course not."

"I can do it." Insistent, he brushed away her hands to take care of the task himself. The next thing he knew, he was holding the third button in his fingers.

"Nice work. Now do you feel better?"

Aaron's temper got the best of him. "Why don't you get married and have a dozen kids so you'd have someone else to drive crazy."

For a moment Abby's guard dropped and he saw her surprise and hurt; then the professional mask slipped back in place and she withdrew to take the clean shirt out of its protective dry cleaning bag.

Aaron could have kicked himself for his tactlessness. "I'm sorry."

"No, you're not."

"I only said it as a joke."

"Well, let me remind you of something, Aaron. If it wasn't for the hours I'm able to dedicate to you and this office, you'd be lost."

"I know." He sighed and downed the rest of the juice hoping the gesture would in some small way help remove the tension lines forming around her mouth. She had pretty lips; on the thin side, but soft and rather vulnerable-looking. Rising, he finished unbuttoning his shirt and, tugging it out of his pants, he slipped it off. "As a matter of fact, I wouldn't mind if you were as full of advice about the girls as you are with things here in the office."

"Oh, no." Though she didn't look up from her task, Abby shook her head with unmitigating decisiveness. "When it comes to children, I'm as much of a novice as you are."

"How can you say that? You're female, they're female..."

"It's not quite that simple."

"It is to me. You're naturally nurturing."

"I'm *what?* Ow!"

Aaron tossed his stained shirt on his desk and reached for the hand Abby was shaking. "What happened?"

"It's nothing. I only stuck my finger on this safety pin holding the customer number to the collar."

Though she tried to extricate herself from his hold, Aaron held fast. "Let me see." He turned her hand to inspect the scarlet period punctuating her pale skin. Without a moment's thought or hesitation, he lifted her hand to his mouth.

"Aaron, what are you...?" Abby gasped at the first stroke of his tongue and gave an even harder yank.

"Will you hold still? I'm only trying to stop the bleeding. See?" He held up her unbleeding finger for their mutual inspection. "All better. No, I got that wrong." Once again he brought her index finger to his mouth, but this time to bestow a kiss. "There. Now it's all better."

With a final desperate jerk, Abby succeeded in freeing herself. Her expression was priceless. Well, well, he mused, it was about time. After five years he had finally managed to get under her image-perfect reserve and reduce her to speechlessness. He was delighted. And—as if there were such things as bonuses for moments like this—when she recovered enough to break eye contact, she suddenly didn't seem to know where to look.

After her gaze skimmed his bare chest a second time, she snatched up his clean shirt, shook it out and held it up for him to slip into. Aaron could sense embarrassment radiating from her in every stiff movement she made. Yes, this was very interesting. Abby possessed a natural grace, and under normal circumstances she treated him with as much sexual awareness as she would bestow on an old hound. He couldn't have thought of a more entertaining—not to mention intriguing—way to get his mind off his troubles if he had tried.

After slipping his arms into the shirt's sleeves, he extended his wrists towards her. Unfair or not, he wanted to prolong the moment. "Can you do these for me? It'll go faster," he explained, when all she did was stare at his unbuttoned cuffs as if she were viewing the lethal jaws of a creature she expected to snap at her.

"Uh . . . sure. Of course."

At first he was disappointed that she kept her eyes carefully focused on the task at hand. But no matter, he amended after a moment; there were other appreciative signs giving away her lost composure. "You know I don't think I've ever seen you blush before. Interesting . . . and at your age, too."

"What do you mean 'at my age?' Thirty isn't exactly ancient."

"It is for blushing, considering I was only performing a little first aid."

"You had my finger in your mouth."

"I did that to Dee only yesterday when she burned herself on the iron."

"I'm not a child and—oh, Aaron, what do you mean she burned her finger? She's only seven, she has no business being near electrical appliances in the first place."

Resigned to the realization that his respite from his worries was over, Aaron let his head fall back and sighed at the ceiling. "Tell me something I don't know. But there's only one of me and three of them. She wanted to make a stained-glass painting or something by melting crayon shavings between wax paper. Before I discovered what she was up to, she'd burned herself. That reminds me, I'd better call Mrs. Kaminski and warn her not to use the thing until I get it cleaned. I forgot to do that because by the time she showed up I was running late. You see what I'm going through? They're driving me out of my mind. As soon as I think I'm making some progress with them, something happens and they reinstate this cold war on me."

"Give them time, Aaron. They have to be feeling extremely vulnerable right now."

"I know, and I am trying to be tolerant. Good grief, it was my suggestion they come down here, wasn't it? But they're treating me as though I'm the villain in all this. I tell you, Abby, the way things are going I'm going to be living in a padded cell before the month's over."

While Aaron stepped into his private bathroom to finish buttoning his shirt and tucking it into his pants, he heard Abby pick up the juice glass and his soiled shirt. "You underestimated how much work three children can be, that's all," she called from the utility room. "What you should have done is arranged to take some time away from the office so you could focus on them. In fact, it's still not a bad idea. Why not move up your vacation and take them someplace?"

"Abby, this is Miami, tourists come here for their holidays. Besides," he grumbled, emerging from the cubbyhole, "why would I want to leave the comfort of my own home?"

"Because it's *your* territory, not theirs. Right now they don't need the reminder of that."

"It's not bothering them as much as you think. Mitch has locked me out of my Mercedes twice already, Jenna's on the phone so much with her friends back home that the phone company's probably going to declare a windfall profit off of my bill alone, and Deirdre is single-handedly out to destroy every appliance in the house. They're not feeling unstable, believe me." However, when Aaron noticed Abby's unblinking look, he grimaced. "Oh, all right, maybe you have a point. Maybe it would help if I looked into taking some time off now instead of later. At least I'd be able to keep a better eye on them. But I still don't understand why you want me to take them somewhere. Why can't we stay home and just do whatever comes to mind?"

"Because the idea is to help them get their minds off troubles at home."

Unfortunately it made sense, but just as Aaron was about to admit as much, his phone buzzed. He leaned over the desk and punched the lit button on the display panel before snatching up the receiver. "Yes, Delores?"

"Judge Bainbridge would like to know if you could come over to his chambers before you go into session?"

"Tell him I'm on my way." After hanging up, he gave Abby a fatalistic shrug and headed for the door. "This will have to wait—Bainbridge wants to talk. Where'd I leave my jacket?"

Abby crooked her finger and led him back to her office. But before Aaron could reach for the misplaced item, she dangled his tie before him. While she slipped it around his neck and expertly knotted it, Aaron smiled at the woman who at five-ten in heels still stood inches shorter than him. "You take good care of me."

"Someone has to," she murmured, smoothening his shirt collar over the tie. "You're always taking on more than is healthy for you to handle."

For a moment Aaron felt a familiar yearning for the domesticated, family-oriented life he'd always believed he would have, but had never gotten around to acquiring. Something always seemed to get in the way or take precedence. Work mostly.

Things couldn't be much different for Abby, since she was right about how busy he kept her. Despite everything, though, he found it damned easy to visualize her in something softer... lacy... or sheer. Face it, he thought his amusement growing, not everyone saw domesticity as a Norman Rockwell drawing.

"Does that mean you're going to look into this vacation business for me?" he asked, using his most engaging smile.

She pursed her lips, but Aaron could tell she was softening. "I knew this was going to fall into my lap. Why did I open my mouth?"

"Because even though you try to hide it, deep down you have a soft spot for me. Admit it—the thought of seeing me with egg on my face upsets you. Some day we'll have to play Freud and analyze why."

"It's easy enough to figure out," she drawled. "You sign my paychecks, remember?"

He lifted her chin and reconsidered her mouth. "How brave you get when you know I'm forced to beat a fast retreat. I wonder what you'd do if—"

Abby's phone rang, cutting him short. Aaron dropped his hand. Just as well, he told himself. He had almost erased the lines between their professional and personal relationship. It had been enjoyable, even exciting. But the complications...

"Do me another favor and get the notes I've drawn up on the Hendrix case out of my briefcase?" He snatched up his jacket, intent to make his own retreat. "I think there's a precedent that ties in with this, and the case was tried right here in Florida. See what you can find. Oh, and Abby..." He'd reached the door and glanced back at her. What the hell, he thought. "Your new shampoo? I like it."

Abby stood rooted in the same spot—even after Aaron was gone and the phone stopped ringing. She knew she looked like an idiot with her mouth open and her hand halfway to her hair, but it was several more seconds before she succeeded in shaking herself out of her trance. No, her clamoring nerves confirmed, she hadn't just imagined the last few minutes. The man she'd trained herself to see strictly as her boss, one of Miami's most esteemed criminal-court judges, had abruptly, completely destroyed her carefully established method of dealing with him. Aaron had forced her to think of him as a man.

Unbidden, the image of his dark head bowed over her hand flashed before her eyes, and once again she could feel his lips and tongue against her skin. A tingling sensation rushed through her, leaving her body feeling hot and clammy, despite the refrigerated air blowing down at her from the vents above her head. She'd always known that if she ever let him get under her defenses, it would be like this; that was why she had always been so careful. Why hadn't she been careful this time? What made today different than any other?

Because today he actually let down his guard and showed you how vulnerable and desperate he was feeling.

Idiot, she chided herself, fool. The last time she'd volunteered to be a human bandage, she had become Mrs. Brad Richmond. That should have cured her of believing compassion or even affection could be foundation enough to build a lasting relationship. It certainly hadn't been enough to keep her marriage from crumbling.

Abby bit her lip and wandered over to the wall where beside her own diploma hung several photos of Aaron with state and national dignitaries. In each, he was the dominant presence; it was those discerning gray eyes and his lean, intelligent face, that could switch from looking elitist to feral in the time it took him to strike his gavel in court—and then boyishly appealing when he was relaxed and untroubled by the responsibility of the office he held.

From the day she'd come to work for him, she had realized that it wouldn't take much effort to fall in love with Aaron Mathias Marshall. As a result she'd opted to treat him like a slightly eccentric distant relation rather than the charismatic dynamo the media labeled him. She had a feeling that though it amused Aaron, he was also relieved. With women constantly throwing themselves at him at the various functions he was obliged to attend, the last thing he needed was a starry-eyed groupie right in his own office.

"So snap out of it and get to work," she scolded herself.

She picked up his briefcase and brought it next door where she placed it on his desk. Removing the work he'd taken home over the weekend, the scent of sandalwood and lime rose from the leather case and created havoc with her determination to concentrate. Small wonder he had noticed the citrusy scent of her shampoo; he preferred the crisp freshness of it, himself.

When she'd located the folder documenting the case he had referred to, she scanned his notes. His handwriting was bold, the letters well-defined. Like the man. Would he make love with the same boldness? Abby shivered as her wayward thoughts created a vivid image where she was on the receiving end of such concentration. But just as quickly, she muttered an indelicate imprecation and returned to her own office.

She wasn't going to allow herself to start doing this. Nothing sensible would come of it—except to jeopardize a job she loved. If her wayward thoughts were intent on concentrating on Aaron, she would do as he'd asked and find him and the girls someplace to go on vacation. Someplace that would be fun and unique, a memorable experience for all of them. And while they were gone, she would do well to take a long, hard look at her life, count her blessings and remind herself that she'd better keep her capricious imagination under control.

"Make a fool of me once, shame on you," she muttered remembering the old saying. "Make a fool of me twice, shame on me."

* * *

Abby didn't see Aaron again until late afternoon. It was past four when she heard the private door to the courtroom open and shut. Grabbing her steno book filled with her notes of the day, she hurried to his office.

"How did it go?" she asked, as she always did while he slipped off his black robe and hung it in the closet. She already had a hunch what his answer was going to be, but even with his mouth drooping at the corners, she could not deny he cut an impressive picture.

"You know what the trouble is with our new assistant district attorneys? Their boss. Just last week I reminded Syd Wendell that it wasn't my responsibility to educate his young guns in the rudiments of law, so what does he do? He lets his newest kid take over Patterson's case because Patterson's been reassigned to the Chambers murder that's on the front page of every newspaper in town. From Patterson to a puppy...I swear I feel like a damned dentist who's spent his entire day pulling molars with his bare hands."

Abby did her best not to grin. "But think of that assistant D.A. He probably sweat out the seams of a brand new suit brooding over the prospect of facing *you*. I'll make you a cup of herb tea," she added, heading toward the coffee maker where she had recently made a pot of hot water. "You'll feel better when I tell you about the vacation options I came up with. It took me most of the day, but I think you'll be pleased with the results."

From behind her, she heard Aaron groan. "How could I have forgotten? Damn. I'm sorry, Abby. I should have stopped you before you went on such a wild-goose chase.''

She paused midway in pouring the steaming water over the tea bag she'd set in the mug. "What do you mean?"

"When I went over to see Dick Bainbridge this morning, I happened to mention my problem, and he came up with the perfect solution. He'd leased a houseboat for a Mississippi River cruise. It's two weeks, starting right after this Fourth of July weekend. The problem is that his eldest daughter's just decided she's getting married then. There's some hitch about her future husband being transferred out of the country—anyway, what with one thing and another, he was going to have to cancel and lose his deposit. Instead, we've made a deal. He's going to let me take his place and we're going to switch vacation schedules."

"A houseboat up the...?" Abby set down the pot, as well as the mug. "Do you think the girls will go for that? I was thinking along the lines of something like Disneyworld or—"

"Amusement parks," he scoffed. "This is education. Imagine following the path steamboat pilots traveled a hundred years before...communing with nature...dining on freshly caught catfish...why just yesterday I caught Mitch trying to fish out goldfish she'd dumped into my pool. At the time I wasn't thrilled that she'd used all my shoelaces and my tennis racket to make a rod and line, not to mention wondering who in the neighborhood was missing pets out of their aquarium, but now it all seems to have been a message, doesn't it?''

"Maybe, but . . . Aaron, you're talking about taking three children on a huge river. You don't know anything about boating. You live on the canal and you don't even own a boat. How are you going to—to navigate?"

"What's to navigate? The Mississippi runs north and south. The boat is a pontoon or flat-bottomed job or something, and Bainbridge said the people at the marina can fill me in on whatever else I need to know once we get there."

Abby shook her head. Her normally levelheaded, conservative boss had been bitten by an adventure bug, thanks to Judge Bainbridge's talent for exposition, and he was picturing himself as something between Mark Twain and an Indiana Jones adventurer. "No, no, no," she replied, seeing it was her duty to remain the voice of reason. "You're not thinking this through. What about the girls? What are they going to do while you're preoccupied with steering this houseboat?"

"Why they'll be wide-eyed with wonder, taking in all the scenery."

"I mean twenty minutes after you cast off."

Aaron's lips flattened into a grim line, creating an expression Abby had seen too often to find intimidating. "They can always take turns steering with me."

"Okay. Why don't we leave that for a moment," she suggested, seeing her current approach was leading her nowhere. "What if one of them falls overboard? You won't be able to watch all three at once, and as you've already pointed out since the moment they arrived, that's a full-time job even on dry land."

"Bainbridge says there are protective railings, and that life jackets are supplied because they're mandatory for minors."

That was something, at least, but Abby still didn't know how he was going to handle three little girls on his own. "You seem to have given this some thought, but have you considered what you'll do if there's a storm, if you have mechanical problems? And what about the mundane things, like cooking and making sure each of you has enough clean clothes? And what if—"

"Hold it. Hold it!"

Aaron came over to her and took hold of her upper arms. The physical contact would have sent her pulse skittering if it were not for the self-satisfied smile on his face. What now? she wondered.

"I agree. You made some very good points. But, Abby, give me some credit. I've thought about those things myself, and I think I've come up with a great solution."

"Aaron, Mrs. Kaminski already warned you that you're going to either get her help while the girls are staying with you or pay the higher premiums when she increases the coverage of her medical insurance. I don't think she sees a houseboat ride up the Mississippi as a negotiable item."

"I wasn't planning on taking, Mrs. Kaminski," Aaron replied with a dismissive shrug. "I'm taking *you*."

Chapter Two

"Do you have an alternative plan to toss a burlap sack over my head and carry me on board? Because that's the only way you'll get me to go with you, Aaron."

Abby could tell by the bewildered look on his face that this wasn't quite the reaction he'd been expecting. How typical of confident and charismatic men who possessed a talent for making the world rotate around them.

"What do you mean? It'll be perfectly safe. I'll make certain of that."

"That's not what I was addressing, though for your information there have been those who've said as much and weren't around long enough to eat their words."

She had to have a sign stamped across her forehead reading "gullible." What else would explain her track record? Human doormats must exude a fragrance uniquely attractive to men such as Brad and Aaron.

Squashing the fleeting spasm of joy she'd experienced at the thought of not having to spend her vacation apart from him, she shrugged out of his hold and stepped away from temptation. No, she was damned well not going to fall deeper than she already had and that was final.

"I don't understand," Aaron replied, looking dumbstruck.

"You don't understand the word no?"

"I don't understand why you'd turn me down flat like this."

"Well, they say there's nothing like a good night's sleep to clear out the cobwebs."

"But you love boating," he said persisting, as though logic alone could clear up this glitch in his plans. "You used to tell me how you and Brad would— Oh."

The children must, indeed, be getting to him. Normally, his perceptivity was far more keen. He was, however, right on target now; she had adored those days when Brad wasn't at practice or doing a celebrity appearance, and she and her former professional-football-playing husband chased the sun on their cabin cruiser. The wind would feel glorious as it whipped through her hair, the sun's rays would warm and seduce…but her favorite moments had been when Brad would coax her below to their cabin to make love. At least, they had been her favorite until she discovered she wasn't the only one he was taking down there.

"Too many painful memories, I suppose?" Aaron murmured, thought it wasn't actually a question.

Abby shook her head. "I'm over the hurt. It's just that I'm angry at what a naive fool I was. I'm sorry, Aaron, but my answer remains the same. I can't help you out of this dilemma."

"But you have to. Abby, I need you."

Ah, yes, the ultimate bait. She had been wondering when he would dangle that tempting morsel before her; after all, it had a history of working so well. Like Pavlov's dogs' conditioned responses, she'd been trained to react predictably upon hearing those four magic words. Only what Aaron didn't seem to comprehend was that she was out to cure herself of the bad habit once and for all. He soon would.

"Correction, you need a sitter, a nursemaid, a cook and a disciplinarian," she replied, ticking the items off her fingers. "You need an entertainer and, undoubtedly, a laundress. What you refuse to understand is that none of those are in my job description. For forty-nine weeks out of the year I'm virtually at your beck and call. But you're not going to manipulate me out of my vacation."

"Manipulate? You're making it sound like a sentence of hard labor."

Close, she thought, considering she would be restricted to, spending twenty-four hours a day in a most contained and, therefore, intimate environment with a man she was trying to remain indifferent to.

"It would be fun," Aaron continued. "Where's your spirit of adventure?"

"Safely under lock and key, where it's going to stay until you shove off, Skipper."

He raked his hands through his thick dark brown hair. The uncharacteristic assault on the immaculately groomed mane told Abby he was fast approaching frustration. "I thought you liked children," he shot back.

Expected as the retaliation was, pain still pierced through Abby like a dagger aimed for her heart. She reached behind her, gripping the edge of his desk to steady her suddenly weak legs. How dare he say that, she seethed. Better than anyone, he knew how much she loved children, *wanted* children. He had been with her the night she'd lost her own baby—not Brad, but Aaron.

Vivid memories from the night of her accident flashed through her mind, as if the wreck had occurred last week instead of four years ago. Once again, she saw herself emerging from the courthouse parking garage; she saw the oncoming sedan skidding in the rain; the blinding lights, as it aimed into her car like a bullet shot from a high-powered weapon. She remembered rising out of blissful oblivion to find Aaron hovering over her, wrapping her in his raincoat and murmuring reassuringly, words she couldn't focus on because the wrenching pain in her abdomen was too great.

It had been Aaron who rode with her to the hospital and he who stayed until she'd been wheeled into the operating room. He had still been there when she awoke and learned she had lost the baby she'd been carrying for three months.

"That's not fair," she whispered hoarsely.

Looking aghast at himself, Aaron muttered something under his breath and stepped toward her. With an energy Abby didn't know she possessed, she spun around knowing if he touched her, she would shatter like the thinnest hand-blown crystal. Wrapping her arms around her waist, she prayed he would have the sense, if not the compassion, to realize as much. She hadn't cried since that night, not even when she separated from and divorced Brad; she didn't intend to start now.

"Abby," Aaron whispered, his breath tickling the fine hairs at her nape. "That was a damned foolish thing to say, and I'm sorry for my thoughtlessness. The fact of the matter is—I do need you. There's no way I'm going to be able to pull this off alone."

"You should have thought of that before you told Judge Bainbridge you'd take the boat." She knew she was being obstinate, but her own tender feelings had yet to stop stinging from his careless response. On the other hand, she couldn't deny she was touched, even mollified by his sincere apology, as well as his sheepish admission.

Don't you dare weaken now. His is the oldest ploy in history.

"True, I should have. But you know what they say about hindsight and—hey, wait a minute, partner." Aaron reached around her and cupped her chin, forcing her to meet his wary, if apologetic, gaze. "Am I missing something here?"

There was the understatement of the century, Abby thought with an inner sigh.

"Are you trying to tell me that I inadvertently made a mess of some other plans you've made? Is there someone in your life I don't know about, Abby?"

Here's your big chance, Abigail. Don't waste it.

But when she found herself drowning in the bottomless gray depths of his eyes, saw the crooked smile that wouldn't quite stay on his firm lips, Abby felt the opportunity slip away as surely as sand escaping through splayed fingers. Would he actually care if she said yes? Was there concern, even regret in his gaze, or was she simply feeding an overactive imagination again? She had less trouble gauging her reaction to his touch. He was stroking the line of her jaw with his thumb, and the pads of his fingers—slightly rough because of all the work around his house he preferred to handle himself—were as masculine and seductive as any caress could be.

"No," she heard herself admit. "I haven't committed myself to anything yet."

Yet? That's priceless. You haven't dated a handful of men since your divorce.

Besides, that, her only relatives lived on the other side of the country and seemed content to keep it that way. Commitments, indeed.

"Then won't you reconsider?"

His voice, always appealing because of its rich tenor quality, now possessed the added allure of sounding disarmingly gruff. Oh, Lord...how she wished he was asking her something else, like inviting her out for something that wasn't work-oriented or a favor.

"I don't know, Aaron," she said, hedging to buy time. At least she did have the sense to sidestep him and pretend a need to check his desk calendar.

"The girls like you."

"You can say that, based on two brief meetings? They barely said a dozen words when you got stuck in court and I picked them up at the airport for you."

"But on Saturday, when you stopped by to bring over those games for them, it made an impression. Dee said you were nice, and the other two have a tendency to use her as a guidance system, whether they admit it or not."

"Right. They were so impressed, Mitch still refused my offer to braid her hair."

"She doesn't let anyone touch that mop. You should hear this—she says her hair works as an antenna and if it's too neat all the signals she receives get messed up."

Abby couldn't keep from giving in to the smile twitching at her lips. "You're making that up."

"From the mouths of babes, Abby. You should hear some of their ideas. I don't know why Sean hasn't considered writing a treatment for a sitcom about them."

"He probably figures everyone would think the characters were unrealistic."

They laughed and for a moment everything was back to normal, comfortable and open. And yet not. Abby couldn't keep her heart from interfering with her thoughts. She also would not let herself forget that Aaron was too much of a tactician to resist taking advantage of her better mood.

"I have an idea," he said, right on cue. "Why don't you come over tonight? I promised the girls we'd grill dinner outside. They want hamburgers and corn on the cob. It's not fancy fare, but it would give you a chance to be around them a bit more before you made up your mind."

Desperately trying to ignore the leap of her pulse, she quipped, "I thought I had."

"Abby." Aaron groaned. "Do you want me to beg?"

She wasn't asking for miracles, nor was she greedy. Just noticing that she was more than a means to an end would be sufficient. On the other hand, what if this was her opportunity to make him see her in that light? Maybe if they spent more time around one another outside the office—not that she would ever consider throwing herself at the man, of course—he would realize she had more to offer than what he'd noticed so far.

She moistened her lips. "I guess I could come over for a while."

"You're an angel." He rounded his desk. "All I need to do is go through these messages and then I'm off to the market to pick up some odds and ends. What time do you think you'll be able to get out of here?"

Abby indulged in another brief fantasy, imagining how nice it would be to go to her apartment and change into something more casual and feminine. Just as quickly, she abandoned the idea. No sense in being disgustingly obvious. "Five-thirty? Six at the latest."

"Fine."

He scooped up the stack of pink phone memos she and Delores had piled there during the course of the day. Abby watched, admiring his trim physique, his strong yet artistic hands, so tanned against his crisp white shirt; how characteristic that despite his grueling day, he managed to look fresh and in control. If only he would say something more personal, such as "I'm looking forward to spending more time with you outside the office" or "Gee, Abby, this is going to be a wonderful opportunity for us to get to know one another better." Instead, he tossed several of the memos into the trash basket and, reaching for the phone, began dialing the number listed on another memo.

With an inner sigh, she headed back to her own office. *You're still too romantic-natured for your own good, Abby. You might as well be wishing for snow, a blue moon or a magic lamp.*

"Mitch, put down that can of lighter fluid...the spatula, too. We don't flip charcoal, we use that to flip the hamburgers. Jenna, honey, if you eat all those chips, you're not going to want dinner. Where's your sister? Dee? Jenna, go find your sister. Mitch, come back here with my spatula, you little..."

Aaron gave up trying to keep order and glanced at his watch. Speaking of missing persons, where was Abby? It was six and there was no sign of her. The burgers were ready to go on the grill, Jenna had devoured half a bag of chips, as though Mrs. Kaminski had locked her in a closet all day, and he was getting dangerously close to indulging in a second Scotch to calm his nerves. If he ever needed Abby's talents for making things run smoothly, he needed them now.

"Uncle Aaron, I know where Dee is," Mitch said, returning from wherever to tug at his pant leg. He was glad he'd had the foresight to change into jeans; glancing down, he spotted a streak of charcoal from her filthy fingers, remnants of when he had caught her digging in the bag of charcoal.

"Where?" he asked, prying the spatula out of her other hand. For such a gamine-faced, adorable runt, she was a holy terror and she had the grip of a starving python.

"In your office."

"Oh, hel—Help," he amended quickly. "Uh, Jenna, watch your sister for me. I have to go inside for a moment and check on something I forgot to bring out."

"No, you don't. You're going to go punish Dee," the eldest of his nieces replied.

She tossed back her flowing locks with a mature flare that had Aaron sympathizing with the little boys who, all too soon, would be lining up to try to win her affection. Like Mitch, her hair was a vibrant chestnut brown, but unlike Mitch's it had been painstakingly brushed again and again until it fell halfway down her back in glossy waves. Also like Mitch, her face was sweet and pixieish, featuring a short turned-up nose and toffee brown eyes that had just enough of a slant to remind him of a fawn. But while Mitch's eyes sparkled with mischief, Jenna's glinted with animosity.

"I thought you said we were supposed to make ourselves at home?" she continued, her child's voice accusatory.

"You were . . . I mean you are. But Dee knows she's not supposed to be in my study."

"She just went to play some games on your computer."

The problem was his computer didn't have any games programmed into it. Abandoning this latest attempt to reason with the child, Aaron bolted inside. "Dee!"

He was at the hallway when the front doorbell sounded. Swearing, he yanked it open, tossed a, "C'mon in. I'll be right with you," over his shoulder and continued racing down the hall. "Deirdre Marshall, you'd better not have messed up any of my files or your life won't be worth—"

Aaron froze in the doorway and stared at the seven-year-old sitting arrow-straight in his swivel chair, pecking out letter after letter on his computer's keyboard. Her concentration was so intense, he could see teeth marks on her lower lip, which was already bitten to an overripe berry red. She finished the line she was typing, before turning to gaze back at him through gold wire-framed glasses. Dee's eyes were shades darker than her sisters', and the wisdom they exuded made her appear years older than she was. But just like her sisters, her hair was a glorious chestnut, only she usually confined hers to two tight braids.

"What are you doing?" he gasped, trying to catch his breath yet look casual as he slid his damp-palmed hands into his jeans' back pockets.

"Writing Mom and Dad."

"That's admirable. Ever hear of pencils and paper?"

"I thought they'd take me more seriously if I typed it."

Behind him, he heard Abby clear her throat. At least, he thought it was Abby he'd let in at the front door. Did he dare turn around and view her expression? He already felt like the beast of the century. If he spotted even the slightest censure in her eyes, it would just about finish him off for the day.

Aaron rubbed the back of his neck. "Dee, I don't mean to criticize your motives, but you've failed to take into account a key issue here. You should have asked if you could use my computer. It's an expensive piece of equipment and it has a lot of important information on it that I need for my work. Understand?"

"I did ask."

"You . . . you did?"

"When you were scraping up the hamburger meat Mitch dropped on the floor. Remember? You were putting it in another bowl to wash it off and you said—"

"Never mind." He didn't need to be reminded of a moment when he hadn't been thinking his clearest; he had been preoccupied with trying to salvage the main course of their dinner. "Regardless of what you think you might have heard me say . . . I mean—"

"I can stay with her until she's finished," Abby said from behind him.

So she had been the one at the door. Aaron shot her a grateful look over his shoulder, which lasted only as long as it took Dee to give him her opinion of the idea.

"I don't need anyone to watch over me."

"Then I'll sit in this chair," Abby replied, easing around Aaron, "and finish going through my mail. This way I'll be close, in case you do have a question." She sat down and tried to make a few pieces of junk mail look worthy of her perusal.

Aaron noted other things, as well. She had changed, sort of. She wasn't wearing her jacket and she'd removed the bow at the throat of her blouse. Without her glasses, and with a few buttons undone, she looked more relaxed and approachable. Soft. He wanted to tell her how nice she looked, that he truly was glad she'd come, but a scream from the kitchen cut him short.

"Uncle *Aaron*— Jenna slapped me!"

"Give me strength," he muttered.

Abby waved him off. "Go on. We'll be fine."

"I owe you a drink," he told her, as he headed for the kitchen.

It was another twenty minutes before he had things back under control, the hamburgers grilling and the girls safely grouped where he could keep an eye on them. He could not, however, take full credit for the achievement. A great portion of his success was due to Abby. Her presence alone created a change. Like wily forest creatures sensing a trap, the girls were highly suspicious of her, but their innate curiosity also made it impossible for them to ignore her.

She was aware of it, he could tell by the subtle, wry smile that kept curving her generous mouth, and the way she often lowered her dark lashes to hide the amusement twinkling in her usually serene eyes. One of Abby's many strengths was being sensitive to other people's feelings, and she possessed an astonishing ability to overcome adverse situations. That was why, when she had rejoined them on the patio with Dee in tow, he wasn't surprised to see her take out a compact sewing kit from her purse and proceed to replace a button that had come loose on her jacket. It took him only a moment to understand what she was up to. Within minutes the calm, thoroughly domestic chore had drawn the girls and all three were hovering around her like curious, if wary hummingbirds.

"That's one of the more fun things a needle and thread are useful for," she said, ending a tale about puppet-making. "Of course having a puppet is no fun without having an audience to perform to, and being an only child that was often my situation. You girls don't realize how lucky you are to have each other. But you don't need more than one person to have fun making a popcorn-and-cranberry garland for a Christmas tree."

"I'm never going to have anything to do with needles and thread," Jenna announced, though she'd chosen to sit closest to her and hadn't taken her eyes of Abby's hands. The kid had good taste, Aaron mused. Abby had lovely hands, slender and as expressive as a dancer's.

"No? Why ever not?"

"I just won't," Jenna replied with an abrupt shrug. "I like to listen to music and watch TV. But we're not allowed to do that once *he* gets home."

Aaron didn't have to look up from the grill, to know he was the offending party in this part of the conversation. But before he could defend himself, Abby chuckled and shook her head. "You must be planning to be an actress when you grow up."

Looking uncertain as to whether she should be flattered or insulted, Jenna lifted her chin and announced regally, "Actually, I haven't decided yet."

"Oh, barf," Dee muttered, pretending to shove her finger down her throat.

"I wanna be a mommy," Mitch offered, twisting her arms into a contortion that made her resemble a chubby pretzel.

"That's a wonderful thing to want to be," Abby declared, rewarding her with a warm smile. "Do you practice playing mommy with your dolls?"

With a five-year-old's solemnity, Mitch offered an immediate nod.

"She does not," Dee scoffed. "She plays with stuffed animals, not dolls, and she runs over them with her bike so she can stick bandages on them."

"Do not!" Mitch cried, furious.

"Do so!"

"Uncle Aaron! Dee says I hurt my dolls."

"Animals, you mental gnat."

In retaliation, Mitch leaned toward her sister. Just in time, Aaron saw she intended to sink her teeth into Dee's arm, and he swept his youngest niece up into his arms. "Hold on, wildcat. I think it's time to wash those filthy hands, because we're going to eat, okay?"

"I don't want to. I want Mommy," Mitch whimpered, burying her face in his shoulder.

"That makes two of us, kiddo."

"I want her *now*. Mommy!"

Her cry crescendoed into a wail. Tempted to let loose with a yell or two himself, Aaron glanced at the rest of his crew. The mention of one of their parents had his older nieces looking grim themselves.

"Since dinner's about ready," Abby said, pushing herself to her feet, "I better see to setting the table. Who's going to help me?" She didn't get one volunteer. "Jenna, why don't we girls take command?"

The girl ignored her, concentrating instead on a sudden necessity to retie her left sneaker.

"Jenna," Aaron warned, fast approaching the end of his patience.

"I'll help," Dee groaned, throwing herself toward the screen door. "But that means I don't have to help clean up, right?"

Abby shrugged. "Fine with me."

"Hey, she asked *me*," Jenna said bolting after her sister.

"I wanna, too," Mitch said, writhing when Aaron didn't put her down fast enough.

As all three children raced inside, Aaron met Abby's droll look. "Don't say it."

"Say what?" she asked wide-eyed.

"You're thinking it's always like this."

"No, I'm thinking that with some popcorn and peanuts we could have a full-fledged circus going here. Luckily, that doesn't faze me. I happen to work with a man who makes this seem like a picnic."

As she executed a smart pivot and followed the girls inside, Aaron felt the strongest urge to whip her around and plant a hard kiss on her sassy mouth. One of these days, he promised himself, he would give in to one of his impulses. Then let his prim, efficient Abby make what she would of that.

"What did Uncle Aaron do to the bad man?"

Abby used the opportunity of having Mitch's full attention to dab ketchup from her chin. "Well, after the jury found the bad man guilty, your uncle struck his gavel down like this and said in his deepest judge's voice, 'I hereby sentence you to jail.'"

Aaron rolled his eyes at how she had theatricalized his work, but he couldn't help feeling somewhat flattered, too. If Abby really thought he was half the heroic figure she made him out to be to these kids, his ego would need tethering in no time flat. Logic, however, forced him not to fool himself into believing she did.

"Is the bad man still in jail, Uncle Aaron?"

He nodded. "A big jail with enormous walls and giant locks."

"Would you put me into jail if I was bad?"

"No, only for being boring," Dee muttered.

Aaron intercepted Abby's conspiratorial wink. Now, she seemed to be suggesting, was as good a time as any to tell them his news. Did that mean she'd agreed to come along? There was only one way to find out.

He took a last vivifying sip of his drink. "Speaking of being bored, girls, I think I've come up with a solution."

"We're going home?" Jenna asked with a hopefulness that was depressing.

"Er—no. We're going on vacation."

Mitch gave a whoop of joy. "Disneyworld!"

"No, not quite," Aaron said, refusing to acknowledge another of Abby's delicate coughs. "I thought we'd do something more adventurous and, well, educational. You like adventures, don't you, girls?"

"Uh-oh," Dee groaned. "Why do I know this is going to be a drag?"

"We're going on a cruise up the Mississippi River." When he failed to get any response, at all, Aaron tried again. "We're renting a houseboat. For two weeks. Just us and Old Man River, himself." If anything, the silence grew more profound. Even the birds seemed to stop singing. He scowled. "Well, don't everybody stand up and cheer at once."

"I'd rather go to summer school," Jenna announced.

"I'd do your homework, if you had any," Dee promised.

Only Mitch took the idea into consideration, finally asking, "Would we be close to where Mommy and Daddy are?"

"Of course not!" her sisters replied in unison.

Aaron dropped his head into his hands and groaned. This was the end. He was giving up. Maybe he had promised himself that he wouldn't call Sean and Betsy unless there was an emergency, but as far as he was concerned this constituted one.

"I'm actually looking forward to the trip myself," Abby offered in a clam, nonchalant way.

Everyone, including Aaron, stared at her. She handled being the center of attention well, he thought. She almost managed to keep her hand from shaking as she scooped up the last of the chocolate mousse, Mrs. Kaminski had made for their dessert. Licking her spoon clean was a nice touch. Very spunky.

Mitch leaned toward her. "Is he making you go, too?"

"Er, no." Abby's tongue made a suspicious foray inside her right cheek. "I just like to see new places. When I was small like you, there wasn't much opportunity for that, because my family was poor."

"That means she's going along to help watch over us," Jenna muttered, slumping in her chair.

"What makes you think that?" Aaron asked conversationally. "Maybe she's going to watch over me."

Dee wrinkled her nose. "It's worse than we thought," she told her sisters. "They're dating. First Mom and Dad don't want us around so *they* can be alone, and next these two will want all kinds of privacy."

Abby didn't squirm in her chair, but she looked anything but comfortable. Aaron couldn't blame her; he was ready to toss all three of his charges into the guest room and send for a locksmith to put in a dead bolt. How was he ever going to apologize to her?

But to his amazement, she was the one who recovered first. "You're wrong, Dee, we're not dating. It wouldn't be appropriate, since your uncle is my boss. And I don't have to go, if you girls think I'd be intruding on your time with him. I just thought, since the opportunity existed, it would be a great idea—and, of course, I'd be willing to carry my share of the workload."

Dee's head came up with a jerk. "What workload?"

"Oh, chores," Abby replied with a casual shrug. "Everyone chips in and helps on a boat. That's what makes those kinds of trips fun. Think of it, no specific bedtimes, no fussy meals, lots of exploring..."

"Could I fish?" Mitch asked.

"We'd buy you a rod the minute we land in New Orleans," Aaron told her, almost afraid to acknowledge the flood of optimism spreading inside him.

The child pretended to have to wrestle over her decision before she nodded. "I guess I could go."

"Traitor," Jenna muttered.

"Well, it's not like we have a choice," Dee reminded her. She shot Abby a sidelong look. "You weren't just saying that stuff about helping out, were you?"

"I gave my word."

Dee gave her older sister a fatalistic shrug. "Looks like they've got us where they want us."

It was past nine when Abby told Aaron she thought it safe to take her leave without being labeled a deserter. The girls were now upstairs plotting heaven only knew what. He had to admit the house was blissfully quiet, as she collected her purse and jacket and headed for the front door. Still, as he followed, there were ambivalent feelings churning inside him. He knew he'd taken up more than enough of her free time, but he couldn't help notice that everything had gone all the more smoothly while she had been around.

Outside, it was dusk, and Abby's pale hair glowed with silver highlights from the street lamp near the driveway. Her skin, always as pale and pure as porcelain, was made more so by the subtle shadow of fatigue he noted around her eyes.

"Are you sure you wouldn't like a nightcap before you go?" he asked, leaning one shoulder against the doorjam. "You certainly earned it."

"You know I don't have a tolerance for alcohol. If I indulged in anything else, I'd pass out, and you'd have another mouth to feed in the morning."

He wondered what she looked like in the mornings, all drowsy and rumpled from sleep. "You know what they say—the more, the merrier."

Though she chuckled, Abby shook her head. "No, thanks. As fond as I am of peanut butter and jelly, I'm not partial to it as a breakfast staple."

"Mmm. You do look more like the crepes type to me, and it would be nothing less than you deserve."

Her surprised look had him studying her more closely. Did she really not know how much he appreciated her? Counted on her? How strange. He thought he told her often enough. All right, maybe not in actual words, but surely in manner...

"Well, good night," she murmured, fidgeting with her things until she located her keys. "I had a nice time."

"Fibber. But thanks."

"No, really. It was...interesting. I learned a lot of things. Mostly, I now have a new perception of you."

"Dare I ask if that's good or bad?"

"It's not bad, at all."

Her eyes were luminous sapphire pools and her mouth...dear heaven, what would be wrong if he bent and tasted it? Just brushed his lips across—

"Uncle Aaron, Dee won't give me my bear!"

The bear was in deep trouble, and he wasn't so sure about the fate of the rest of his brood upstairs. What did Abby think of this interruption? Was that disappointment he saw flicker in her eyes? How tempted he was to find out.

"Uncle *Aaron*."

Abby took a step backward. "You'd better go. Duty calls."

"Duty. Right. See you in the morning, then." He waited for her to get a few feet away. "And Abby?"

She spun around. "Yes?"

He couldn't help it. He didn't like that she seemed so eager to get away from him. "Sleep well," he murmured. Only then, did he softly shut the door.

Chapter Three

If New Orleans had been a lady, her condition would have been listed as critical. Outside the airport, they found the humidity level was running neck and neck with the temperature, and the temperature was breaking new records; even the breeze was labored. Aaron flagged down a taxi, while Abby kept counting heads and luggage, and tried not to think about how her cotton shirtwaist dress was melting to her body faster than shrink wrap around a package of stew meat. Never again would she complain about Miami's weather. She acknowledged it also would help to revise her definition of dressing "light."

What hadn't helped was that the flight from Miami had been fraught with tension. Mitch had been restless, and intent on examining everything; Jenna had raised their increasing concern because she had kept venturing back to the rest rooms—that is until Abby

noticed the preteen boy several rows behind them and
restricted her to her seat. But Dee had been the undis-
puted nerve-racking champion; she spent the entire trip
staring out the window voicing her concern over the
amount of vibration in the jet's left wing. Before they'd
flown thirty minutes, both the people in seats in front
and behind them had asked for earphones so they
could listen to stereo music and block out her chatter.

Things could only get better, Abby assured herself,
as Aaron succeeded in getting a taxi driver's attention.
She could see that he, too, was hot and ready for a cool
drink and a more peaceful environment. Yet, as travel
worn as his short-sleeved blue shirt and gray slacks
looked, that didn't stop her heart from flip-flopping
whenever she glanced his way.

She still couldn't believe she had agreed to do this.
Two weeks away from the courthouse with him...and
company, she amended, grabbing for Mitch, whose
interest was abruptly drawn toward a woman carrying
a cat in a travel case.

They crammed into the taxi, with Aaron in the front
and everyone else in the back. Abby sat on her left
hipbone to accommodate an indignant Mitch, who insisted she was too old to sit on anyone's lap. Finally,
however, they were on their way and getting their first
close-up view of the Crescent City.

From the air, Aaron had pointed out to the girls how
it was surrounded by Lake Pontchartrain and the Mississippi River. Now he indicated the levees, explaining
how they had long been used to protect the low city
from its higher water levels. Abby thought their presence gave the crowded and seemingly ancient build-

ings an even more vulnerable quality. Most of the poorer dwellings looked about as substantial as matchboxes, while the more stately buildings reminded her of Roman relics, ghostly with their chalky whiteness.

"Look at all the doll houses!" Mitch cried, reaching across Abby to flatten a pudgy and sticky hand against the window that had gone too long without having a close encounter with a paper towel and cleaning liquid. "Can we go play there?"

"That's a cemetery," Dee told her, in her usual superior tone, as Abby removed Mitch's hand from the glass.

Mitch stared, round-eyed with wonder. "What happened? Did they run out of room for the dead people under the ground?"

"That's how they do it here," Dee replied, clearly relishing the opportunity to resume her lecturing. "In the old days, every time it flooded, bodies would pop up out of their graves, so now there's a law that you have to be buried in those above-ground things."

"Says who?" Jenna demanded, ever suspicious.

"The magazine in the front seat pocket of the plane. I read it while you were making goo-goo eyes at that kid."

"I was not!"

"Were, too."

"Girls." Aaron shot them a warning glance over his shoulder. "Could you keep it down? I'm trying to explain where we're going to our driver."

Though Abby had her suspicions that nothing short of a translator was going to make their Vietnamese driver understand them, she did her best to keep the girls preoccupied. "Look inside those courtyards. Beyond the iron gates. See the fountain and all the flowers? Isn't that lovely?"

"Everything looks moldy," Dee replied. "I'll bet they have spiders and bugs as big as my hand." Along with her theory, she formed her fingers into a claw and aimed for her older sister's face. Jenna squealed and, in retaliation, tugged Dee's glasses down her nose. "Hey!"

"Jenna, that wasn't nice," Abby said, retrieving them for the temporarily blinded child.

"She started it."

"I don't like big bugs," Mitch said, her face puckering.

Abby gave her youngest charge a reassuring pat on her thigh. "I don't think you'll be seeing any quite as large as Dee described."

"We were supposed to get my fishing rod."

The imp had a one-track mind, Abby thought with an inner sigh. "True, but we can't go shopping with all our luggage, can we?"

"Uncle Aaron promised!"

"Ssh. He'll keep his promise, only you'll have to wait until we get to the boat, okay? Now look at that horse and carriage down that street. See? The horse is wearing a straw hat with flowers around the brim."

Jenna gave a scornful snort. "I've never seen anything more ridiculous in my life."

"Oh, yeah? Guess you haven't looked in the mirror lately," Dee replied benignly.

That earned her an elbow in the ribs, which she returned with even more gusto, starting yet another round of squabbling. Abby blew a strand of hair out of her face before intervening. What she wouldn't give for some handcuffs and muzzles right now.

"When are we going to get there?"

"We're not. We're lost."

"I vote we fly back to Miami. At least we had a TV there."

Aaron did his best to ignore the comments coming from the back seat, but although they were mostly whispers, his growing tension had made his hearing all the more acute. He ground his teeth together and stared at the map Dick Bainbridge had given him. It had seemed clear enough back in Miami; of course, back in Miami he hadn't thought about having to deal with a driver whose English was limited to "airport," "gotcha" and a smattering of downtown hotel names.

Still, there was no reason to panic—yet; though he would give a great deal for a dark, quiet room and silence for about thirty minutes, anything to ease the tension headache beginning to pound at his temples and the base of his neck. Thank goodness for Abby. He resisted another impulse to glance back at her. At least she was managing to stay in control. Women were simply better at this sort of thing.

It amazed him how cool and feminine she managed to still look in that mint green dress, her hair clipped back in a sporty ponytail. He should have complimented her when they had first picked her up at her apartment. But one of the girls had been acting up, then, and the opportunity was lost. He would tell her later, after they were at the houseboat and things were calmer. If their kamikaze driver got them there without killing them all in a head-on collision, he amended, wincing as they once again cut across oncoming traffic to make a sharp turn.

"Aaron...!"

He didn't blame Abby for her concern; he was certain his toenails had just made permanent imprints on the insides of his loafers. "It's all right," he reassured her, with as much confidence as he could summon. "I'm sure we're almost there."

Twenty minutes later—and only by accident—they spotted the sign indicating the turnoff to Cajun Cal's Marina and Rentals Unlimited. Aaron reminded himself that when Bainbridge gave him the address, he'd eyed the name with some skepticism; pulling up before the flamingo-pink cinder-block building, he wished he had followed his impulses and asked the eccentric senior justice a few more pertinent questions.

After they got out of the cab and their luggage was unloaded, he paid the driver—an amount he gauged could finance the man in establishing his own fleet—and assured himself that the boat they were leasing was no doubt behind the building identified as a "club, general store and bait shop." None of the dubious relics secured to the visible side of the marina looked as though they could get fifty feet from land without some serious bailing or the aid of a bilge pump.

"Get a load of this place," he heard Dee whisper to Jenna.

How could he reprimand her, when she had voiced his exact thoughts? Aaron eyed the dozen or so boats tied to the floating dock. Boats was a generous word, since most of them were little more than crafts with eggbeater-sized motors. The few offerings that were larger looked as if they hadn't seen a good scrubbing or painting since Jean Lafitte abandoned his lucrative pirating career to aid U.S. troops in the battle of New Orleans.

Abby appeared at his side. "Are you sure this is the right place?"

He didn't answer her right away because he had decided to ask their driver to hang around a few minutes, just in case. But even as he turned to do so, the taxi shot up the driveway. Fanning away the cloud of dust it kicked up in its wake, Aaron reminded himself he wasn't superstitious, nor did he believe in omens.

"It's the name Dick Bainbridge wrote down for me." The four pairs of eyes locked on him telegraphed varying degrees of skepticism and censure. "Come on girls, cheer up. Our boat's going to be a beauty. Judge Bainbridge always goes first-class. Tell them, Abby."

"He does when he vacations with Eloise. Was she supposed to accompany him on this trip, or was this going to be one of those expeditions he takes with his cronies?"

He had forgotten about that small technicality. "I'm not sure," he admitted, the weighty hand of dread regaining its hold around his throat. His expression must have mirrored his doubts, because Abby abruptly picked up one of their two Pullman cases and shoved it into his hand.

"Right." She handed each girl her own knapsack, before picking up two tote bags. "Well, we're here, so we might as well find out the rest of the good news."

Watching her ponytail flick with every step of her brisk march, Aaron slung the last tote over his shoulder, hoisted the other heavier Pullman off the ground and followed her and the girls across the steaming asphalt. Abby, he decided, had a unique talent for dry wit.

Entering the store required a descent of two steps, both of which Aaron nearly missed because it was pitch-black inside. It took him several seconds to adjust to the darkness, and when he did begin to notice his surroundings, he realized he'd braked just in time to keep from running over the girls. After a few more seconds, he began to delineate the glow from a blue neon sign on the far wall advertising a local beer. And then came the smells. Aromas assaulted his sensory receptors with a vengeance. Whatever it was that had crawled in here from the bottom of the ocean, escaped its time capsule or aged beyond perfection, Aaron was convinced he could live a full and happy life without making visual contact with it.

"Phewey!" Jenna announced in a loud whisper. "What died?"

"The owner, I'll bet," Dee intoned.

"It kinda smells like the goldfish bowl I used to have," Mitch piped in. She tugged at Aaron's pant leg. "Ask if they have fishing rods, Uncle Aaron. I bet they do."

He gave her a reassuring pat on her shoulder and peered at the blur of white he was beginning to realize wasn't a refrigerator, but an enormous man in a white T-shirt. "Hello, er, are you by any chance Cal?"

"Depends on whether you're spending or collecting."

Wheezing laughter filled the nooks and crannies of the cavernous room and somewhere a can of something tipped over. Aaron's eyes finally adjusted enough for him to see that the man was indeed an image to behold. He stood almost as wide as he was tall, a human pyramid with a head as small and sweet-faced as an infant's. When he laughed, ripples of excess flesh quivered from his neck downward like a mud slide in progress.

"Well, don't be shy," the human pyramid declared. "Come on in. I'll buy you a cool one, while you're making up your mind what it is I've got that you can't live without. Little ladies, how about a root beer float? My freezer's up and died on me and I gotta do something with all the ice cream before it melts."

All three of the girls accepted at once and raced to claim bar stools.

It was indeed a bar, Aaron realized, not a diner counter, or a drugstore soda counter. "Uh, girls...I don't think it's appropriate for you to sit there."

"Aw, let 'em be," their host replied. "My regulars ain't due for another hour or so. No harm done. Where're you darlin's from?"

"Baltimore," Dee replied.

"Miami," Mitch corrected.

"Baltimore via Miami," Jenna told him with a regal lift of her head. "We're visiting our uncle. That's him back there. Do you have hot fudge? I'd prefer a hot fudge sundae."

"Sugar, what I *got* is root beer floats. Tell you what, though, I'll toss in a bag of popcorn. Ain't that a deal? It's yesterday's, but y'all'll hardly notice." He glanced over their heads at Abby. Leered, Aaron noted grimly. "Miami? Say, you wouldn't by chance be with Judge What's-his-name's party?"

"Aaron Marshall," Aaron supplied, not sure whether he should be relieved or insulted. "I'm the one Judge Bainbridge called you about. I'm glad to know we found the right place."

The man disappeared around a corner for a moment and returned with a dripping container from which he scooped out several soupy spoonfuls of vanilla ice cream and plopped them into three tall glasses. "As far as I know there ain't another Cajun Cal in these parts."

"And our houseboat is ready for us?"

Cajun Cal spend a moment impressing the girls with his ability to pour bottled root beer from assorted heights, then behind, beneath and across various parts of his anatomy. Finally adding a shot of whipped cream from a can and plopping a cherry in each glass, he presented the drinks to his enthralled audience.

"The houseboat," Aaron repeated. "Is it ready?"

Cajun Cal scratched his protruding belly, his answering gaze catatonic. "Kind of."

"And exactly what does 'kind of' mean?"

"It means I've got good news and I got bad news. You ready for that beer, yet?"

"No, thank you."

"I think I'd like one," Abby said, stepping forward to claim the stool beside Mitch.

Cajun Cal's expression brightened as though some-one had just turned on a 150-watt bulb inside him. Beaming at her, he set a bottle of beer before her, then snatched up a glass from beneath the counter and wiped it off with the end of his T-shirt.

"Oh, I don't mind drinking from the bottle," Abby assured him.

"No problem, ma'am. Service is what we're known for. Are these your girls? My...you certainly don't look old enough to be anyone's mama. Now if there's any-thing else I can get you—"

"Our boat," Aaron suggested, having heard enough. Maybe he spoke more tersely than necessary, but the big jerk was about to salivate over Abby.

"Your boat..." Cajun Cal glanced toward the doorway leading to the back of his store and rubbed a beefy hand over his several-day-old beard. "I reckon, I neglected to tell you about our little mishap, didn't I?"

"What little mishap?"

"Terrible situation, just terrible. I was robbed a few days ago. Sonofa—" Cajun Cal caught himself just in time and shot Abby an apologetic smile. "Er, s'cuse me, ma'am. What I meant to say was that the alleged perpetrator sort of absconded with several days provi-sions from my cooler, ten cases of beer and my best rental."

"Are you saying the houseboat we reserved is no longer available?"

"Yes, sir, that about sums it up."

Aaron shut his eyes. This couldn't be happening. "Why didn't you phone and tell us?"

"Well, I thought he'd be back by now. He don't usually stay gone this long, no sir. Course, he did take more beer than he usually does."

"Wait a minute." Aaron shook his head trying to make sense of what he was hearing. "You mean you *know* the perpetrator?"

"Aw, it probably ain't right to call him that. I was speaking through my temper, you might say. See, he's my brother-in-law. Worthless wretch if you ask me, but my wife's sorta partial to him, cause he's the youngest and she helped raise him, and all."

Abby swiveled around on her stool and held out her bottle to Aaron. "Maybe you'd better have a swallow or two of this."

It wasn't funny. There was a decided twinkle in her eyes, but Aaron promised himself that if she so much as uttered one peep, a choked laugh or otherwise made it be known that she was amused, he was not going to be held responsible for his actions.

He did, however, accept the beer from her. Gulping down a long swallow, he wiped the back of his hand across his mouth and asked, "Just what do you suggest we do now? We were expecting to cast off just as soon as we stocked provisions."

"Oh, that's all taken care of," Cajun Cal replied, pouring the promised popcorn into three bowls. "Let the girls enjoy their drinks and I'll take you out back to show you the *Ultimate Solution*."

"That remains to be seen."

"That's the name of my own boat. Ain't it catchy? I made it up myself. It came to me a while back, the first time the IRS got on my nerves, to be exact. One day I locked up the place and me and Mona took off up the river for a while in this comfy little flat-bottom that I took in an IOU swap. Mona wanted me to name it after her, but I had my heart set. Got her personalized license plates for her pickup, so she's stopped griping."

This had to be a dream, Aaron thought. Any moment now he would hear the flight attendant reminding everyone to fasten their seat belts for their approach to New Orleans. But even as Aaron assured himself of that, he took a determined step toward Cajun Cal. To do what, he had no idea. The man was at least a half foot taller than his own solid six feet and outweighed him three to one. Still, it was the principle of the thing. He wanted, needed retribution.

"Ah, Cajun—Mr. Cal. Sir," Abby said, sliding off her stool and situating herself between Aaron and the counter. "Could Judge Marshall and I take a quick walk around this—the *Ultimate Solution*? Naturally, we wouldn't want to inconvenience you or your wife..."

"No problem. She's over in New Iberia helping our youngest with the new grandbaby, and I got a room out back that'll suit me fine. Come on and I'll show you around."

If she were not here witnessing this for herself, Abby decided she would never have believed such a farce could happen outside a television sitcom. Their corpulent host led them down a hallway now better lit than the store, to the back, where they just barely missed stepping in something they could only hope was melting ice cream. The girls, declaring they were not about to be left behind regardless of their tempting treats, brought up the rear.

Outside, the heat struck them anew and things looked no more promising than before, when they'd first arrived. The dock was little more than a series of treated plywood boards secured to oil drums. It bobbed and weaved with every step and Cajun Cal's weight alone sent them into a frenzy of motion.

But it was when Abby saw the *Ultimate Solution* itself that she began to wonder how much longer she could contain her impulse to burst into hysterical laughter. Every fantasy she had had about a romantic getaway, every thought about a few stolen moments with Aaron came to an end as she stared at the tuna-can barge before them.

It wasn't that the boat didn't look seaworthy; at least it was floating. But Abby couldn't help noticing that the silver-and-white box-shaped houseboat was much smaller than she had anticipated and far less—luxurious.

"Notice how almost the whole thing is protected by a roof," Cal pointed out, diving straight into his sales pitch. "You'll be glad you have that when it rains. Of course, this being July, I ain't suggesting you can expect a lot of downpours. But it helps to be ready. And look here . . . this is the helm. You just go through that door behind there and lookee, you're back inside."

"There's only one bedroom," Jenna pointed out after a quick inspection. Her speaking glance, however, was for her uncle. Aaron had promised that since she was the eldest she would have her own room.

Abby could see that, to his credit, Aaron was keeping a fine rein on his temper. Nevertheless, when he turned to Cajun Cal, his sarcasm was unmistakable. "My niece has a point."

"Yes, sir, that's a problem, I admit. But check out the accommodations in that room. We've got a full-sized bed for you and the missus, plus bunk beds for the kids. See, we often have our own come by for a visit, so we know about improvising."

"They're not married," Dee announced with the bluntness only the young could get away with.

Abby wanted to put a muzzle on her. She ignored Cajun Cal's intrigued stare and shot a meaningful glance toward Aaron, who missed it because he was pinching the bridge of his nose. "We could always head back to the airport and see what flights they have available going back to Miami," she suggested, mentally crossing her fingers.

"Good idea," Jenna muttered.

"I second the motion," Dee added, then blanched when she intercepted her uncle's stare. "Uh...but I'm sure sorry things didn't work out."

Only Mitch looked upset at the thought of leaving. She insinuated herself between her sisters and her uncle and again tugged on his pant leg. "We can't go yet, Uncle Aaron. I haven't caught a *fish*."

Oh, no, Abby thought, as she watched him crouch down to consider the child. Granted, Mitch was adorable when she turned on her charm, but surely Aaron wasn't going to break down and sentence them all to two weeks on this floating albatross... would he?

His silence dragged on forever. Finally he sighed and rose. "We'll take it," he told Cajun Cal, who broke into a relieved smile. "*Provided* you'll make sure the tanks are topped off, and at your expense, since this isn't what we agreed to in the first place. In the meantime, we'll see about getting the rest of our supplies and load our luggage."

There were dollar signs in Cal's eyes as he met Aaron's steady gaze. "Well, now fuel's a bit high these days..."

"Take it or leave it."

"Then again, right is right. Go on in to the shop, your Honor, Judge, and help yourself. We've got everything you can think of wanting. Browse to your heart's content and I'll fix you up here."

Abby followed one delighted and two dejected girls down the dock. When she was several yards away from the boat, she paused, knowing Aaron wasn't far behind her. "Are you sure about this?" she asked, trying to keep her voice low, so as not to be overheard by the girls.

"Hell, no. But I didn't fly all this distance to accept the first little defeat that came my way."

"'Little?' Since when did you indulge in understatements?"

He ducked his head and ran a finger over his left eyebrow. "Okay, so it's not so little. The question is, are you still with me, Abby?"

What undermined her, was that he actually looked worried. Damn the man for knowing how to get under her skin. "Someone is going to have to save you from mutiny. But you're going to have a hard time selling your enthusiasm to them," she muttered, tilting her head in the direction of the girls.

"Mmm." Aaron placed his hand under her elbow and led her into the store. "In that case, we'd better get in there before they try to hide our luggage."

Chapter Four

Abby stored away the perishables she and Aaron had purchased, placing them in the refrigerator and freezer, but decided to leave the canned and dry goods for later. She wanted to rejoin Aaron at the front of the boat. He and Cal were going over operational procedures, the engine and various check systems, so Aaron would know what to do in case there was a mechanical problem. He could have changed first, she thought coming through the screen door and spotting the men as they crouched down to peer under the helm. If he had, he wouldn't have gotten his clothes stained with dust and what looked to be oil smudges.

Watch it. You're sounding just like a wife.

Giving herself a mental shake, she shut the door behind her and listened to their conversation. What impressed her was hearing how fast Aaron was grasping instructions. Well, why not? He was always handling his own chores and repairs around his house; dealing with a boat was not all that different. But that still didn't answer a recurring question, namely why he chose to live on the canal, yet not own a boat himself?

From around the corner, she heard squabbling, and she went to investigate. The girls were arguing over their life preservers, for no discernible reason other than to burn up some energy, Abby noted, since the vests were identical. Let them wear themselves out, she thought shutting the storage box they'd retrieved the vests from. She crouched to assist Mitch with her straps. The faster they grew exhausted, the sounder they would sleep tonight.

No sooner did she have Mitch safely secured than the child announced, "I have to go to the bathroom."

"Michelle Marshall..." Exasperated, more with herself than the child, Abby chuckled. "It serves me right for not thinking of that myself."

She shepherded the entire trio off the boat and back to the store, determined not to get caught by such a maneuver again. When they returned she coaxed them back into their vests and rechecked everyone's straps. It wasn't easy convincing the girls that they would have to wear them all the time except when they were in bed.

"It's hot," one complained.

"It's too big," another protested.

"It's orange!" Mitch declared, surprising everyone with her new aversion to the color.

This was, Abby sensed, really part of something deeper. She did not need a medical or psychology degree to understand that the girls were actually vocalizing their fears and frustrations over their parents' problems. All she could do was fight these outbursts with as much tender, loving care as she could.

Pointing out that the color was necessary to attract attention in case of an emergency, she explained to Mitch how wearing a despised color was preferable to being overlooked if something happened.

"Like what?" the child challenged.

Abby wasn't about to succumb to her inimitable curiosity. "Never mind," she drawled. "Just trust me, orange is the color you need."

"Guess you're set to take off," Cajun Cal announced soon afterward. He shuffled his bulk toward the dock. "If you'll get the anchors, I'll toss you the ropes from the dock."

Aaron headed for the one in the front of the boat and Abby automatically went to retrieve the anchor in the back. She invited the girls to help, thinking it was a perfect way to get them involved; however, the two eldest refused outright, and even Mitch hesitated. But as soon as Abby started working the winch, Mitch deserted her recalcitrant sisters and raced over to take over the cranking.

"It's so *easy*," she cried, pleased with herself. "I thought it would be hard, and look at all the vegetables we brought up with it!"

"Vegetation," Abby corrected, struggling not to laugh.

By the time she and Mitch had plucked the lengths of greenery from the anchor, Aaron started the engine. The outboard motor coughed to life, chugging out a few spurts of blue gray smoke before struggling into a less labored idle. Abby showed Mitch how to secure the mooring ropes Cajun Cal tossed over the railing, and explained how keeping them neat and out from underfoot was another safety precaution. She spoke loud enough for the other girls to hear, hoping that even if they didn't want to participate, they would learn something.

Finally, they were edging away from the dock. "Come wave goodbye," Abby suggested, as the big man saluted them. Jenna and Dee stood rooted where they were, arms crossed and lower lips thrust out. They looked like a pair of bookends. It wasn't easy stifling her frustration, but Abby explained with as much patience as she could, "It's the least you can do to thank him for those ice-cream floats."

With long-suffering sighs, they came to the railing and unenthusiastically joined in the waving. "If we don't get back, send the coast guard!" Dee yelled, cupping her hands to her mouth.

"Dee, really." Abby glanced over her shoulder, glad to see that Aaron was out of sight at the wheel. He probably hadn't heard. She so wanted this trip to be a success for him. He was trying hard, yet so far few things seemed to be working out the way he had planned.

They weren't more than a few hundred yards from land, when the two older girls abandoned the positions and headed inside.

"Where are you going?" Abby called after them.

Jenna spun around and planted a hand on her hip. "Where do you think? We're going inside where it's cooler."

On the contrary, Abby had found the metal building was as hot as an oven. "Why don't you stay outside. You don't want to miss all the scenery."

"You're not our mother and we don't have to do
everything you say!"

The screen door slammed shut behind them, leaving
Abby feeling like the most wicked of witches north,
south, east or west. Common sense told her she
shouldn't take their rejection personally, but it stung,
nevertheless. Feeling a tug on her skirt, she glanced
down to find Mitch watching her, her gamine features
puckered into a troubled frown. "You can go with
them if you'd like," she gently assured the child. "It
won't hurt my feelings."

"They said Mommy and Daddy are giving us away,"
the five-year-old said, her voice trembling. "If they
don't want to be married anymore, does that mean they
don't want us?"

"Oh, sweetheart." Abby crouched down to em-
brace her. "Your parents want you very much. Only
they're having some problems at the moment, and they
need time to work them out by themselves. They explained that to you, didn't they? The reason they sent
you and your sisters down to stay with your Uncle
Aaron was because they didn't think you should hear
all that."

"You mean they're yelling and stuff?"

"I doubt it. From what your uncle tells me, your
parents aren't like that. No, they're probably taking
long walks and talking about different things. In a way,
it's like going back to when they were first dating.
They're getting to know one another again."

"Why? Mommy's the mommy and Daddy's the daddy."

"True." Abby smiled. "But they're also husband and wife. Being busy at their jobs made them forget and grow apart."

Mitch leaned her forehead against the railing and considered the subtle wake they were creating. "Daddy growed from us, too," she offered at last.

"He knows, honey. That's part of the reason he's spending this time with your mom. First they need to fix things between each other, and then they can fix things with you and your sisters. But you need to try not to worry. It's a very good sign that they noticed the problem before it was too late."

"I'm gonna tell Dee and Jenna, then maybe they won't be so bad all the time."

Abby blinked away the sudden tears that burned in her eyes. "Michelle Marshall, has anyone ever told you that you're a very smart young lady? Tell you what, let's both go inside. I need to change into some shorts. Afterward, you can help me figure out where to put the rest of our supplies, okay?"

Some eight hours after setting out from New Orleans, Aaron was still high on the thrill of being on the river that Mark Twain had referred to as a "king" and a "hero" and T.S. Eliot had called "a strong brown god." Of course, this tin-and-aluminum eyesore couldn't compare to anything as romantic and noble as a steamboat or as luxurious as the houseboat that Dick Bainbridge had described, but Aaron had long since recovered from his disappointment. The important thing was they had made it; they were on their adventure.

He hadn't told Abby, but as a boy growing up, he had dreamed of doing something impulsive such as this. Always considered the levelheaded, cerebral one in the family, trapped in the image of one who possessed sturdy purpose—as his father often pronounced, with the pride of a man who'd enjoyed watching his likeness duplicated—Aaron had learned to repress his spontaneous side. Sean had been the adventurer in the family, the risk taker, the one who could afford defeats and failures because being the youngest—and somehow never being asked to face the same challenges Aaron did—less was expected of him.

But now he was having his turn, and freedom was a baroque symphony; its tempo strong, lush and lively, as it danced through his veins. He grinned to himself once again recalling Sean's reaction when he'd called to ask permission to take the girls along. Never again would his brother be able to call him "Sir Stable." Aaron had no idea how far north they would get, he didn't even have a clue as to where to set anchor or tie in tonight, but he hadn't felt this excited since presiding over his first case.

"Want some company?"

He glanced over his shoulder to see Abby ducking her head around the screen door and holding up a tall plastic cup of iced tea. Earlier she had changed into olive green shorts and a pink tank top, and though he'd managed to restrain himself from indulging in an impulsive wolf whistle, he was having less success at not staring at her whenever she came into his line of vision.

"You bet."

It was hard to believe this willowy, long-legged vision was the same studious young woman who made his professional life run so smoothly. She looked anything but bookish and businesslike now; in fact she looked positively tempting.

"Thanks," he added when she was near enough to hand him the drink. His watch told him it was almost two hours since they'd had dinner, and the constant wind gusting at him was dehydrating him faster than he had guessed possible. He took several swallows, while Abby considered the view from this part of the boat.

"It's more impressive than I'd imagined. How far have we come, do you think?"

"We're a few miles beyond Baton Rouge."

"Are we making good time?"

"Hardly. The steamboats that used to run this regularly could make Vicksburg in a day, Memphis in two and a half, St. Louis in less than four. Of course, those were race records. We're in no hurry, are we?"

"No, of course not. I was just wondering."

He pointed beyond the rising left bank. "We're entering a more hilly terrain now."

"Are all those vines covering everything grapes?"

"Kudzu. Would you believe I once read about this stuff on the front page of the *Wall Street Journal*? It was brought over from Japan to help against erosion, but it's becoming more trouble than anyone could have anticipated. See how it's climbing up those utility poles and completely covering everything else in its path? Some people say it's taking over the entire south.''

"It's rather artistic though, like the plant sculptures in old English gardens. I notice we're beginning to leave the Spanish moss behind. The girls are glad. They think it looks spooky, but I love it.''

Mention of the girls had Aaron cutting short his wandering thoughts about walking Abby under a tree drenched with the cascading moss and stealing a long, intoxicating kiss. "What are my little angels up to?" he asked with a sigh, as he remembered their gloomy behavior during dinner.

"They're playing a board game at the kitchen table.''

He took another sip of the tea, unable to understand the reasoning of the young mind. "With all *this* to take in?''

"Give them time, Aaron. Jenna and Dee are still in a mood to pout. I think Mitch is coming along, though.''

"She won't be, when I tell her she has to wait another day or so before I can let her try out her new fishing rod. That Cal was a character, but he had the foresight to draw me aside and warn me that some of the river is polluted.''

"How terrible.''

"Well, Louisiana's been experiencing some economically hard times and it didn't get easier when the oil business fell apart. As a result, fewer restrictions have been put on industries, just to keep them here, but it's created problems on an environmental level. The legislature's beginning to realize that. It's been particularly hard on their fishing industry, especially down at the mouth of the river, so regulations are starting to tighten up again.''

"I'm not looking forward to explaining that to her, or the others, for that matter. At their age, all they're interested in knowing is when they'll have a chance to play in the water.''

"I'll find someplace upriver where we can turn in to one of the tributaries and anchor for a while.''

"They'll like that.'' Abby turned away from considering the murky water and returned to the helm to pick up the now empty cup. "How are you doing? You don't look nearly as tired and harried as you did when we first set out.''

"I feel great, better every minute.'

"Better be careful, I'm tempted to believe you.'' She tilted her head and eyed him with more bemusement than curiosity. "This is really fun for you, isn't it?''

"Sure. Well . . . I'm not about to give up law or anything.''

Her expressive eyes widened with mock relief. "Just imagine how thrilled District Attorney Wendell will be to hear that bit of revelation.''

Aaron shook his head and smiled wryly. "Ah, Abby, you're good for me. You keep me humble. Here I am, thinking I'm evolving to this new plateau of personal insight, and you nudge me right off my anthill.''

She shot him a mild look. "Excuse me, but nothing about you can be compared to anthills. That's the point. You never do anything just because it looks like a fun thing to do, which is why this whole trip has me entirely baffled.''

Her first statement pleased him almost as much as it did to learn she'd been spending what sounded like a considerable amount of time trying to figure him out. "Maybe it's time I told you a few deep secrets about Aaron Mathias Marshall."

"Uh-oh. Is this where you confess you didn't graduate summa cum laude, after all?" she teased, crossing her arms beneath her breasts.

Leave it to Abby not to let him get overly melodramatic. With a wry smile, he corrected his course, to stay well inside the lingering wake of the tugboat a quarter mile in front of them. "No, this is where I tell you that despite what you obviously think, I could have easily turned out to be another type of person entirely."

"Hmm...now you are going to have to elaborate."

"I grew up working hard to evolve into the person I am today. It didn't just happen, as it does to some people. I may have been born with a good mind, but I had to learn to be a disciplined student. You see, I wanted to play more sports...take life at a bit more of a relaxed pace...live for more than my studies. My father, however, had envisioned an entirely different scenario for me. Maybe if my mother hadn't died when Sean and I were still so young, she might have coaxed him to loosen up some, but that wasn't the case. Also, I was the eldest; it was an unspoken understanding that if anyone was going to rock the boat, it certainly wasn't going to be me. Don't get me wrong—I like my life and love my work. But every once in a while I get an urge to be more spontaneous and adventurous, like Sean."

"That's not unusual. Don't you think he probably wishes he was more like you?"

"No doubt. Otherwise he wouldn't have turned into a workaholic these past few years and all but destroyed his home life. And you're right, it's normal, part of growth, maybe there's even a touch of sibling rivalry involved, I don't know. I do know that it's when we allow our minds to become stagnant or trapped by tunnel vision that we stop stretching and testing ourselves. What I'm not saying very well is—in a way I've been making as big a mistake as Sean has. It's time to step back and take a closer look at my life, and to reacquaint myself with my family, or what's left of it."

"There's plenty left," Abby murmured. Then she uttered a short, soft laugh. "And here I'd always believed it was a waste that you'd bought a house that not only had a pool but was on a canal."

"I use my pool."

"But you don't have a boat tied to your private dock."

He shrugged, his expression turning sheepish. "There's barely time to keep up the maintenance on the pool, let alone care for a boat. Still, I like the canal because—well, I suppose, like anyone else, I don't want to abandon all the dreams of my youth."

"If you truly believe that, then you won't," Abby gently assured him.

Aaron drew in a deep breath, grateful for her sensitivity. She could have laughed at him—after all, in the scheme of things, his wasn't the most earth-shattering of problems—but she hadn't. She understood and was supportive. It just reaffirmed how right he'd been to want her in his life. As an assistant, he reminded himself, eyeing the horizon that was turning orange with the setting sun.

"Here we are hundreds of miles from the office, and you're still talking shop," he managed to say gruffly. he needed to lighten this conversation before he did something crazy. "What's it take to turn you off, lady?"

"Me?" She looked astonished until she caught his expression, then she grinned. "Oh. Well, you could always try letting me take over for a while," she suggested teasingly.

He cocked an eyebrow. "Why? Thinking of turning this wreck around, when I'm not looking?"

"No, I was thinking that no matter what you say, you have to be getting tired."

Aaron shifted from one foot to another. He had been wishing he had taken time to change into the more comfortable deck shoes he'd purchased for the trip; standing so many hours in one spot was hard on the soles of his feet. "I can always pull back that stool," he said, motioning behind him with his thumb to indicate the chair he'd pushed out of the way.

"Is that a polite way of saying you don't trust me?"

She couldn't be serious? He already trusted her with his career, his reputation, his credibility…and now this latest insight to his mind and heart.

He took a step backward and with a grand sweep of one hand, invited her to move between himself and the helm. When she did, he released the wheel to her; however, he didn't withdraw. Instead, he placed a hand on either side of the console and leaned forward so their cheeks were almost touching. "Have you ever been on a river before?"

"No. But the Atlantic isn't exactly small potatoes, you know."

"True, though what I'm saying is watch the current. You'll really feel it in places. Our friend, Cal, said when you let it turn you too far, it's like a fat, lazy fish nudging you out of its way with its tail."

As he anticipated she would, Abby gave the wheel a harder turn to the right. "Oh, I feel it!"

"And don't forget to keep an eye on those back-view mirrors secured to the railings," Aaron added, finding it far more interesting to concentrate on her profile. She had lovely skin, flushed from the heat and glowing with a fine mist, the result of the humidity and—dare he think it—their close proximity? "When you see a larger vessel gaining ground, you need to move aside and let it pass," he continued. "Especially now that we're past Baton Rouge. The channel's not as wide and deep now. No more than nine feet. Our flat bottom and lighter weight will make it easier for us to navigate shallower water than a round-hulled vessel. But even we need to be careful."

The intoxicating scent of gardenias blended with the citrus fragrance of her shampoo and had Aaron inching closer to draw it deep into his lungs. The movement brought his chest against her back and he felt her tense.

"Have you thought about where we should anchor tonight?" she asked, her usually even-modulated voice sounding wispy.

"Not in the last—thirty seconds or so." He found himself beguiled by the shell of her ear; funny how he'd never noticed that it was every bit as delicate as a pink rosebud. Unable to resist, he awarded it the lightest of kisses.

"A-Aaron?"

"Mmm?"

"What are you doing?"

"Enjoying your perfume."

"I'm not wearing any...at least, not anymore. It must have worn off hours ago."

"No, there's just enough left to make me feel like doing something very—spontaneous."

Abby swallowed. "Well, it's been a day for spontaneity, hasn't it?"

"You'll have to help."

Startled, she glanced back at him. "Help?"

"By not moving," he murmured, his heart beginning to thud as first her breath caressed his skin, then his lips came in fleeting contact against hers. No, he wasn't going to put this off any longer; he was going to find out what it was like to kiss Abby Gordon...take her lips with his and...

They struck something with an abruptness that knocked Abby off balance. She fell back against him and they both went careening into the screen door. From inside came a series of thuds and crashes and several high-pitched squeals. Then Aaron's backside made hard contact with the deck, momentarily making him deaf to everything but the sirens going off inside his ears as pain ricocheted through him like a jackhammer.

He was barely aware of Abby sprawled across his lap, until she squirmed and tried to get to her feet. "Easy!" he groaned, as she reinvented pain for him.

"Oh, Aaron... Lord, I'm so sorry."

"Don't apologize, just keep still a moment."

But she insisted on helping him to his feet. "Are you okay?"

"I'll live. Damn," he muttered, wincing at the ongoing shrieking coming from inside. "Girls?" He opened the door and ducked his head inside. There they were at the end of the hall, huddled together against the cushioned kitchen-table bench. "Hey... what's with all the sound effects?"

"Are we sinking?" Mitch asked, her voice faint and wobbly for someone who had just been wailing louder than any folklore banshee.

"Of course not. We're just a bit..." he glanced over his shoulder at the water. It was moving, they weren't "...stuck. How's everyone in there? Anyone get hurt?"

"No," Dee replied, sounding almost regretful.

"I guess not," Mitch seconded with a sigh.

"A can of soda rolled over my foot."

Aaron couldn't help noting that Jenna's announcement was made with a bit too much enthusiasm. "Soda?"

"A full can. It fell off the counter and rolled over me before I could get up on the bench."

Give me strength. "Try to be strong, Jenna. Abby will be with you in a minute. In the meantime, would you girls please start picking up whatever else fell on the floor."

He withdrew and faced Abby, finding her with her head bowed and her arms wrapped around her middle. "Hey, what's this?" Surely she wasn't crying? he thought, seeing her shoulders shake. His first impulse was to take her in his arms and console her; but wasn't that what got them into this mess in the first place? "Don't worry. We'll get free," he assured her. "I'm sure there's no damage. Abby?" He ducked to see her face and frowned. "You're laughing!"

"Actually," she managed in a strangled voice, "I'm doing my best not to."

"How can you laugh at a time like this?"

"Well, no one's ever run himself aground before trying to kiss me."

"I...*Me?* Who had control of the wheel? Not me."

"But you were interfering with my concentration."

Female logic. Maybe the fates were sending him a message; maybe he had been edging toward a more disastrous calamity. Hell, it would only have been a kiss... wouldn't it?

He raked his hands through is hair. "Fine," he growled. "Laugh, if you find it so amusing." As for him, he was tempted to jump overboard and swim for land, then walk to the nearest asylum and commit himself.

What was wrong with her? What was happening to *him?* Completely confused, he stalked off to inspect this newest headache.

Chapter Five

It wasn't true that things looked different by the light of day, Abby brooded, while waving to the towboat captain who'd just helped them get free. All things considered, she still felt last night's accident had been more humorous than catastrophic. Why did Aaron insist on being so stiff-necked about it? It wasn't as if she had been aware of making that sharp ninety-degree turn toward shore and shallow water. Yet ever since, he'd been scowling as though she had been plotting against him.

"When you deal with an alluvial body of water, you've gotta expect the unexpected," the helpful but amused captain had pointed out upon his arrival. He had barely needed to take in their situation to know what was going on. "This area's generally one of your safest, only we've been having some mighty strong rains up and down the entire Mississippi valley this year, and there's been an endless flow of debris and sand washing in. You found a collection of stuff they haven't had a chance to clear away yet. The thing to remember for the future is to keep an eye on the changes in water. Learn to read it, yep, that's the secret. 'Course, you give it a chance, the old man'll fool you. Nothing it likes better than to create mischief.''

It hadn't been all that bad. So they had spent the night hung on a mini virgin island. Things could have been far worse. Abby had been content to drop the anchors and make the most of the situation, confident that someone would eventually come along to help. They did, too. At the first hint of dawn, the captain's lusty call had roused her and she'd eased from bed, so as not to waken Jenna beside her, or the girls sleeping in their bunks. Within minutes he'd pulled them free. Now they were once again heading north under their own power.

She waved one last time to the *Marti Rose*.

"I think that's the most ridiculous name I've ever heard," Dee muttered, joining her at the back railing. The commotion had apparently awakened her, as well. Dressed in blue shorts and a T-shirt bearing some cartoon character Abby couldn't identify beneath her life vest, she'd emerged without having brushed her hair, nor did she appear to have washed the sleep from her eyes.

Yet instead of lecturing and pointing out that one grump on board was enough, Abby patiently drew the child's hair out from beneath the vest. "Come on, Dee, lighten up. The *Marti Rose* is a lovely name."

"No, I mean towboat. How can he call that a towboat, when he said he's on his way upriver to *push* a barge?"

"Ah. Well, it's because . . ." Abby discovered either her mind wasn't quite as awake as she had believed or the youngster was on to something. "I suppose that's something you can put in your journal to ponder over another day."

"I don't have a journal."

"No? I'm sure I was your age when I started my first one."

"I don't even know what it is."

"It's a diary."

"Oh." Dee was silent for a few seconds. "But why would I want to write some dumb word like that in one?"

"Because you've made an important observation today, and it's worth remembering. Just as this is an important time in your life. Everything you're thinking and seeing, whatever you'll do in the days to come, will determine the kind of person you're going to be when you grow up. Keeping a record of that journey helps you remember your experiences and feelings accurately."

Dee made a face and knocked the toe of her red sneakers against the bottom rung of the railing. "Who wants to?"

"You think so now, because everything looks bleak and you're feeling sad, but someday you'll see that this was also a summer of adventure and fun. That's what life is all about, Dee, good times and bad times all mixed up."

"Life is hard," Dee mumbled.

No kidding? Abby thought, wanting nothing more than to scoop the child into her arms and give her a big hug; however, such an impulse would be premature. But unable to resist completely, she stroked Dee's sleep-mussed hair. "Sometimes, sweetheart. But I've learned that it doesn't make you feel any better to let it get the best of you. Now, what do you say we go see about breakfast? Your sisters will be up soon and I know I could use a cup of coffee. No doubt your uncle will in-hale an entire potful himself."

Dee's frown blossomed into an irreverent grin. "Yeah. He slept on the kitchen-table bench without con-converting it in the way Cajun Cal said to. When I got up to get a drink, I heard him hit his head on the table and say a bad word. It was funny."

Abby cleared her throat. "Maybe, but don't forget the last several days haven't been an easy time for him, either."

"I guess. I sure miss the old days when he used to be nicer. He used to visit our house and he would bring us presents and give us piggyback rides. Now all he does is yell and make rules."

"He's different because he's aware he's bearing a new responsibility for you and your sisters. When he came to visit you in Baltimore, he was the good guy bringing presents and playing with you right? It was your mom and dad's job to tell you to turn off the TV, brush your teeth and go to bed. And be honest, you haven't always been thrilled when they gave you or-ders, have you?"

Dee shrugged evasively. But when Abby remained silent, she finally shook her head.

"See? It's not all that different. For the time being your uncle is the rule maker, only there's a slight hitch. He's never had to make rules for children your age before, and he's having a problem knowing what's the best way to go about it."

"You don't have children and you don't mess up half as much as he does."

"Why, Deirdre Marshall, I do declare that sounds like a compliment," Abby teased, touching a hand to her heart. But when the child looked more embarrassed than amused, Abby abandoned her attempt to keep the tone of their conversation easygoing. "I appreciate the thought," she continued, her tone somber. "But the fact is that unlike your uncle, I have a bit more experience. I was married once, and I almost had a baby."

"You did? What happened? Oops!" Realizing she'd committed an error in manners, Dee clapped one hand over the other on her mouth.

"That's all right. I can talk about it now." She smiled to reassure her. "I was in a car accident and I miscarried. Shortly afterward, my husband and I divorced."

Dee lowered her gaze to her sneakers. "Gee...I guess that made you sad, huh?"

"Very. And I wasn't a particularly nice person to be around, either."

The railing became a practice barre, as the child contorted her slim flexible body this way and that. "What Jenna said yesterday must have hurt, too."

"Only for a few moments. Only until I reminded myself of how homesick and scared she was."

Dee nodded. "I hope you get to have another baby someday. You'd probably make a pretty good mom, because you care and you don't talk down to kids."

Abby had never thought about it before, but bouquets came in a variety of shapes and forms. She swallowed the lump in her throat and smiled. "That's one of the nicest things that anyone has ever said to me. I'm truly touched, Dee." With a last glance toward the *Marti Rose*—more to count her blessings than anything else—she gestured toward the kitchen. "So what do you say? Why don't we celebrate by making everyone a whopper of a breakfast?"

"Uh...I don't think you want my help. I'm not very good in the kitchen."

"I'll let you in on a little secret. We all start out that way. How would you like to learn to be good? You could surprise your mom and dad when you get home with breakfast in bed."

"You think I could?"

Abby winked at her. "Piece of cake."

Women. Would he ever understand them?

It was mid-afternoon and they were approaching Vicksburg. Aaron steered passed a restored paddle wheeler. Docked and empty of passengers, it had a sad ghostlike quality. Above and beyond the cliffs dotting the skyline were modern buildings. The contrasts between the natural beauty of the land, the romantic images of the past and the modern architecture of steel-and-glass office buildings were striking. How different than Natchez with its pine trees and pastel-painted old mansions set high on the bluffs.

But at least Natchez had won the girls' and Abby's temporary interest. Now they were too busy giggling and gushing over—of all things—a bottle of nail polish. Who cared about geography, let alone culture and history? Each was having her turn getting her toenails painted a pale frosted pink. The waste of all these surroundings festered at him until it became impossible to keep silent.

"In case anyone's interested, we're now passing the sight of one of the country's most esteemed national parks." He didn't intentionally mean to sound as if he were reprimanding a courtroom full of rabble-rousers, but all those bare little feet with their shiny pink toes wiggling at him was just too much.

Abby, looking more girlish than womanly with her bouncy ponytail, her yellow shorts and a green shirt tied high around her midriff, glanced up and stared at him as though he'd just materialized out of thin air. Nothing like adding insult to injury, he fumed to himself.

"Girls, I think your uncle has another story to tell us," she murmured.

Groans rose from all three of her devotees. "Here we go again," Jenna moaned. "He only finished the one about that Nacho Place an hour ago."

"Natchez Trace," Aaron ground out, enunciating each word.

"A great historical trail," Dee intoned, mimicking him.

Her sisters howled; Aaron seethed. Fine, he decided, if they wanted to miss out on one of the greatest opportunities of a lifetime, let them.

"Aaron." He hadn't been aware that Abby had left her brood until she was beside him at the helm. "Please don't be angry. They're only trying to cheer you up a bit."

Without shoes, she barely reached past his chin and it made her seem more feminine and fragile. Aaron didn't like how that dampened his ire. "Aren't you afraid your fan club will miss you?" he grumbled.

Tempting lips as pink as her toes parted with her soft gasp. "Why—you're jealous," she whispered.

"Ha!"

"You are." She stepped closer to rest a hand on his forearm. "Oh, Aaron. This isn't a contest. Besides, you're the one who asked me to come along to entertain them."

"Not when I'm trying to pass on some knowledge. One of the most critical battles of the Civil War was fought here."

"But you're dictating history to them. Nothing shuts off a mind faster than being fed dry information."

"Dry? This is fascinating stuff!"

"To you maybe. 'The flags of England, Spain and the U.S. once flew over the city of Natchez, formerly the capital of the Mississippi Territory. It's the southernmost point of the Natchez Trace.' Aaron." Abby sighed. "I hate to be the one to break this to you, but another Mark Twain you're not."

"And who are you trying to be in that getup? Madonna?"

"Their friend, which is what you asked me to be—exactly what I'm trying to be to you, too, you stubborn man."

Aaron didn't understand how words so tenderly spoken and affectionately worded could knock such chinks in his armor. She was supposed to be apologizing for undermining his authority, for inciting a revolution in the ranks. Instead, she was making sense, depressing sense.

"You don't understand. I stayed up until all hours every night last week reading up on these places," he told her, recognizing the man-made inlet that established an island between the river and the city. "For six weeks something close to twenty-seven thousand soldiers and a river full of gunboats fought over this area."

Abby drew a deep breath and nodded. "And one day during a history class the girls will remember they sailed past it and they'll recount what they saw to their schoolmates, bringing it alive for them. They are looking, Aaron. But you're forgetting that they're dealing with their own heartache and priorities right now. It won't work to throw numbers and facts at them, this way."

"Nothing I do seems to be right," he muttered. He shot her a brief look. "You, on the other hand... they're starting to hang on your every word. Why don't you put me out of my misery and share your secret?"

"There isn't any secret. I'm just trying to find a common ground with them."

Aaron glanced down at her slender, elegant feet. Feet like hers should always be shod in strappy bits of leather that showed more than they hid. "Somehow I think I'd look ridiculous in that shade of pink. I don't suppose you have something in a respectable navy or a sporty lime green?"

Her smile was slow but real. "I'm afraid not. But if you found us a place to anchor for the rest of the day and changed out of your judge-on-vacation clothes and into something more approachable, then joined us for a fierce game of 'Go Fish' or 'Simon Says,' I think you'd be making great strides to recoup lost ground."

"With you, too?" At her surprised, wary glance, he offered a self-deprecating grimace. "I'm not unaware that I've been behaving like a first-class stuffed shirt, Abby."

"Not entirely, though I have been concerned with your degenerating sense of humor."

"You're referring to last night."

"I've decided to be magnanimous and admit we were both to blame."

"Big of you."

"Credit it to our long-working relationship. Sometimes a change of scenery makes people behave in ways they ordinarily wouldn't, if they were in their normal environment."

Now he was beginning to follow, and understanding didn't come empty-handed; it brought with it new realizations. "Abby, are you saying you don't believe I really wanted to kiss you last night?"

She looked toward the children, the cemetery and everywhere but at him. "I suppose at the moment you thought you wanted to."

"No doubt due to some spell you'd cast over me that opened my eyes to your heretofore hidden charms. Or did you purchase something in New Orleans when I wasn't looking, a voodoo potion to put in my iced tea, perhaps?"

"I hate it when you start overdramatizing like those TV lawyers."

He had the grace to wince. "Damn, Abby. I always knew you were a tough customer in the office, but you don't pull any of your punches after hours, either, do you?"

"Even fewer. Don't forget you're on my clock."

He wanted to grab her and give her a good shake. More, he wanted to draw her inside where they could have some decent privacy and do something about the strange tension once again mounting between them.

"I wanted to kiss you," he murmured.

"I believed you the first time."

"I *am* attracted to you."

"But it upsets you."

"Why shouldn't it?" he demanded, less quietly. "We've worked together for five years. Where have my hormones been all that time?"

"Like your dreams, redirected toward your career, just as you said yesterday. Also, don't forget I was married. You've always been traditional about such things. Believe me, I not only understand and approve, I'm grateful."

"Never try having a deep discussion with a woman who even knows your voting record," Aaron muttered under his breath. He shook his head, wishing he could figure out what was going on in that sharp head of hers. Normally such conversations were more balanced and give-and-take. Abby was editorializing and little else.

"Why did you laugh?" he added, pursuing other questions.

"I'm not laughing."

"Last night. Why did you laugh?"

"Well, what was left? You already had most of the epithets covered."

His answering look was rife with warning. She really was pushing this evasion bit too far. "At least you didn't run screaming in terror or disgust at the notion of us kissing."

"I was, er, game to try it."

Finally, a crumb! The flutter of her pulse at the base of her throat, however, told him at least a portion more than those meager words and her lash-veiled eyes would.

"Game. Spoken like a dedicated sacrificial lamb," he drawled. "Are you, Abby? Are you placating me, or am I right in my hunch that there's a kindling of something more going on here?"

She glanced over her shoulder. "This may be a good time to remind you that females between the ages of two and ninety have bionic hearing."

"Let them listen. It'll be the first serious attention they've paid me in days." Aaron barely nodded to the waving driver of the speedboat that raced passed them. He found Abby's growing discomfort far more interesting. "That's it, isn't it? Well, I'll be...this isn't one-sided in the least, is it?"

"Could we please table this discussion until a more appropriate time?"

"Let's not. You let me think I was out of my mind, that I was going to have to plant the idea in yours. Now I'm beginning to realize it's impressively fertile territory all by itself. Come on, Abby, confession time. How long?"

"If you'll excuse me, I see my nail-polish wand has about dried to uselessness. I'm going to take it inside and rub it down with polish remover. In the meantime you can try wiping that self-satisfied smile off your face."

He let her get two whole steps away from him before replying, "I'm nowhere near satisfied yet, Abby. But be assured, I will be. We both will be."

When you opened a can of worms, you had to anticipate a few slippery moments. All Abby's analyzing came down to that, as she watched Aaron toss Mitch in a high arc. With a delighted scream, the child plunged into the water. All things considered, at least he was coming around with the girls.

For the second day in a row he'd found a feeder river and they had traveled upstream until they'd come to a spot to anchor and play. The effect this was having on the girls was amazing, even better than she'd hoped. What was more important was that Aaron was regaining his old rapport with them and, as a result, he seemed to be having a better time.

But at what cost to her peace of mind?

She sighed and shifted her deck chair farther under the protection of the roof and out of reach of the en-

croaching sunlight. Even in the shade, the heat was
withering; but as inviting as the water looked, she
wasn't about to put on her suit and join in the fun. The
blue maillot was respectable enough; however, she
knew she could be wrapped with an entire bolt of burlap and Aaron would still look at her the same way,
amused, curious and—she had only to think of it and
her pulse went haywire—hungry.

It was the latter reaction that frazzled her nerves the
most. Granted it was flattering, and no less than what
she'd been dreaming of; but she was too aware of how
long she had been waiting for this to happen not to be
just a little wary. As a result, she wanted to take things
slowly, make sure it wasn't a fleeting attraction that,
like a shooting star, would soon be extinguished, devoured by its own energy.

Now, more than ever, she was grateful for their
somewhat cramped quarters; at least it made keeping
Aaron at arm's distance much easier to accomplish.
Last night, the girls had had so much fun they resisted
going to bed until it was late enough for Abby to excuse herself and go with them. The look Aaron had
shot her would have melted a hole through a safe door,
but at least he had refrained from making any comments. Today, while he'd been at the helm searching for
this spot, she'd again been able to avoid him by keeping busy with chores and entertaining the girls.

"Now me, Uncle Aaron!" Dee yelled, kicking up a
geyser as she raced to reach him.

"Okay, but this is the last time. You girls have about
worn out your old uncle. I'm going to go up on deck
and rest with Abby."

"Abby's not resting," Mitch insisted, while brushing wet strands of hair from her face. "She's reading a magazine."

"Then I'm going to help her read it. Maybe her eyes are getting tired from concentrating so hard."

Dee's response left no doubt of what she thought of that and Jenna hooted. Abby decided she would have to keep a sharper eye on those two; they were more intuitive than she'd surmised.

"Do we have to get out, too?" Mitch asked, her expression anxious. She patted her orange vest. "We have these, we'll be okay."

"I tell you what," Aaron replied, lifting her out of the water to give her a smacking kiss on her round tummy, "we'll lower that raft we inflated earlier and if you girls stay tied to the boat, you can take turns paddling around, okay?"

Clever man. Gorgeous, too, she added, watching him from behind the protection of her sunglasses and magazine. He reached the ladder and hoisted himself out. He might not have an athlete's muscular body, but it was lean and well-toned. She let her gaze wander downward. When she came to his gray swimming briefs, she glanced away. Briefs...he just didn't play fair.

"Now behave and take care of one another," he told the girls, while lowering the yellow-and-blue raft over the side. One by one, he reached down to hoist them into it. "Remember, I'll be watching."

"You'll be talking to Abby," Dee corrected, ever the sly one.

"Believe it or not, I graduated top of my class from Doing-Two-Things-at-Once 101, Miss Eagle Eyes." Aaron handed her the small oar. "Be good, or you'll have me on your team for 'Go Fish' tonight."

"No! No! I promise I'll be good!" she cried, back-paddling away from the boat.

With a shake of his head, Aaron came toward Abby. "Kids." He shook his head, lowering himself onto the foot of her deck chair.

As he raked his hands through his hair and splattered cool water on her and her magazine, Abby lowered her sunglasses and eyed him over their tortoiseshell frames. "Don't complain. Your resemblance in behavior is astounding."

"You're just in a bad mood because we only asked you a half dozen times to join us."

"I was enjoying myself right here, thank you."

"I'm sure. That has to be the third time you've paged through that thing. For a woman who can give one suit a half dozen different looks, since when did you get so interested in fashion magazines?"

"Since I learned where to give one suit so many looks," Abby shot back, her smile benign.

Laughing, Aaron reached behind him for a towel draped on the next chair. The long stretch awarded Abby another closeup view of taut muscles, flat abdomen and the mat of shiny black hair peppering his chest and legs. It was all too easy to imagine herself entwined in his strong arms and pressed close to his powerful body. In desperation, she flipped the page of her magazine, nearly ripping it from the magazine.

"You should have at least put on your suit and dangled those sexy legs in the water."

"Uh-uh," she managed, though her throat went dry at the compliment. "Inevitably, you would have conspired to drag me in. Since I just washed my hair this morning, I thought I'd forego the pleasure."

Aaron draped the towel around his shoulders and leaned over to trace a finger from her knee up her thigh toward the cuff of her white shorts. "It never crossed my mind."

"You're not to fib out of court, either, your Honor."

"Abby, you wound me."

"I will, if you don't stop that." She brushed his fingers away, as she would an irritating fly.

His smile grew into a predatory grin. "Will you get all prim and huffy, if I tell you that I like it when you play hard-to-get?"

"I'm not playing hard-to-get, I'm being sensible. We're responsible for three children, and right now they're watching us with the concentration of television censors reviewing a steamy rock videotape."

"Then, let's not disappoint them." He nudged her knees to one side and inched closer. "Kiss me, Abby. Right here and right now. Kiss me. It's what you want. Heaven knows it's been on my mind day *and* night. Do you know what it's been like laying on that insult of a bed at night and thinking about you in that great big bed?"

"It's not so big. For your information, Jenna sleeps like a bantam prizefighter making a last-ditch effort to defend his title."

"Then why don't you come out and join me. We could come out here...share horror stories."

"Get eaten alive by mosquitoes the size of carrier pigeons."

"You're being stubborn."

"I'm being—"

"Uncle Aaron!" Mitch cried. "Jenna and Dee already had turns paddling. When's it gonna be *my* turn?"

"More important," Aaron murmured, gazing deep into Abby's eyes, "when's it going to be mine?"

Desire kicked the temperature to the sizzling level and Abby wondered at what temperature her clothes would turn to ashes. Something had to give; she'd never felt passion come this quickly or this strong. Still, it would be insane—not to mention wrong—to succumb to it here and now.

"They say the best things are those you wait longest for."

Aaron groaned. "Whoever said it was either a saint or a masochist." With that he hoisted himself from the chair and made a clean dive back into the water.

Abby bit her lower lip as she watched him. Was she making a mistake in not giving him what he wanted, showing him her true feelings? There was no denying he wasn't thrilled with her arm's length behavior, but at the same time she didn't think he was ready to be exposed to her true feelings. If she succumbed to his kisses, that was what would happen. She wouldn't be able to hide the truth from him, and then she would be putty in his hands. She couldn't risk that. Her experience with Brad had cured her of ever being so vulnerable, so foolish again. But, oh—she laid her hand to her stomach, feeling the ache of deep longing in her womb—how she longed to experience the passion she knew Aaron could bring her.

Chapter Six

"All right, partner. Sit down here beside me and prepare to reel in the biggest, fattest, meanest fish in the entire river." Aaron repositioned the newly purchased plastic minnow bucket, the container of earthworms and the shiny new tackle box, to make a place for Mitch. Over the top of her new purple baseball cap, he sighted Abby watching them through the kitchen window. "Hi! We're back. Care to join us?"

"No, thank you. Call me fickle, but I have this thing about getting too well acquainted with the dinner I'm supposed to consume. By the way, I've set out a package of pork chops to defrost, in case your finned friends have other plans for the evening."

"Oh, ye of little faith."

"On the other hand, you may end up thanking me for my foresightedness."

Aaron turned back to Mitch, not even bothering to hide his grin. With every day that passed, this ongoing banter with Abby was taking on more undercurrents than even this river possessed . . . and he was enjoying every minute of it.

They were between Memphis and the Kentucky border, the mid-July sky was dotted with lamb's wool clouds against a backdrop of eye-stinging blue, and the man in the bait house at the end of the dock had just assured them that they couldn't have anchored at a better spot to limit out in fish. The boat was running relatively smoothly, the girls had actually kissed him good-night last night without him having to ask, and Abby...Abby hadn't run off like a scared rabbit. He'd never felt more in tune with his soul; his heart had never been filled with so much promise. Going on this trip, he decided, was turning out to be the best decision he could have made.

"Come on, Uncle Aaron," Mitch pleaded, thrusting her rod and reel into his hands. "What are we waiting for? Show me what to do."

"Right." He set to the task of getting a hook on her line, something he hadn't dealt with since he was a boy. The experts were right though; like riding a bike, you never forget how. "Are you sure your sisters don't want to try this?"

"Uh-uh." Mitch's head shake was emphatic. "Dee is writing in some book Abby gave her and Jenna is listening to her tapes. Besides, Uncle Aaron, we only have the one rod."

Out came the truth. "You could share."

She sat still for a long moment, her head nearly resting on her right shoulder as she considered that. Then she leaned toward him to give him an impulsive hug. The scamp, he thought, she was trying to charm him into getting her own way.

"What are we going to put on first?" she asked, blithely changing the subject.

"How about a minnow?"

Mitch insisted on getting it, which was no easy feat, since it required dexterity and timing, with fish that were even smaller than her Lilliputian fingers. "Got one!" she shouted, withdrawing a wet fish from the bucket. "Now what do we do with him?"

"We're going to place the hook from here to here." Aaron indicated the fleshy area just under the dorsal fin.

With a soundless gasp, Mitch tossed the minnow overboard.

"Hey! What did you do that for?"

She folded her arms across her vest and ducked her head so that all he could see was the purple bill of her hat. "Can't do it, Uncle Aaron."

"What do you mean you can't do it? I just showed you."

"It's gotta hurt."

As if that were not enough to make him feel like the world's worst fiend since Jack the Ripper, Aaron heard a light cough from the kitchen window. Nothing like having an audience, when you were about to squirm your way out of a difficult situation. He didn't need more commentary, he needed advice. "Hold on a second," he murmured, pushing himself to his feet. Stepping over to the window, he peered through the screen. Abby's indigo blue eyes were only inches away. "Any suggestions?"

"Don't use the minnows."

He tapped his palm to the side of his head. "Why didn't I think of that? Of course... only what do you propose I do with them? I don't think the guy who just sold them to me will want them back. I'm his big sale of the day."

Abby glanced beyond him and her eyes began to twinkle with renewed mirth. "Um, Aaron. Don't look now, but I think the problem has ceased to be one."

As fast as he spun around, all he saw was the last minnow going over the side, while Mitch cried, "Hurry! Save yourselves!"

"Aw, Mitch."

He crouched down beside her and she handed him the empty bucket. Never before had such young eyes held so much reproach.

"You should have told me how it was, Uncle Aaron."

"I'm beginning to figure that out, kiddo."

"What's next?"

"How about my last request? I think I'd like a nice cabernet sauvignon with a T-bone, medium rare..."

Mitch wrinkled her nose, before holding the hook between her thumb and forefinger so that it formed a backward question mark. "I mean for this."

He wasn't sure he wanted to answer. "How about we try the worms?"

"As long as we don't have to poke and hurt them, too."

Something clattered in the kitchen sink. Abby, probably in the throws of hysterics, Aaron thought with increasing grimness. "Sweetheart, if we just wrap them around the hook and ask them to stay put, they're going to wiggle off."

"Can you blame them?"

What had he said about enjoying himself, about peace? He eyed the container bearing the worms. Mitch snatched it up faster than a woman at a fifty-percent-off sale and clutched it to her chest.

"Mitch, don't toss the worms over the side. They'll drown. Water isn't their natural habitat."

"Then why were we gonna stick them down there?"

Through the kitchen screen came the sound of Abby humming a song about a gambler who'd learned the hard way about knowing when to fold a hand. Once again, he pushed himself to his feet. This time he extended his hand to his niece. "Come on. There's a place up on the bank where we can set them free. There's grass and moss and rocks. They'll be the happiest worms in Tennessee."

It was fifteen minutes before they were back on board and Mitch actually had her line in the water. But Mississippi catfish—as well as any other variety of finned creature in the area—seemed unimpressed with the artificial worms and lures Aaron had thought quite remarkable when paying for them up at the bait house. What was worse, Mitch was already getting restless. Thirty seconds was her limit after a cast, then she couldn't resist reeling in her line and trying another spot, another lure.

"I don't think this one works, Uncle Aaron."

"Give it a chance honey. The lure's got to be in the water long enough for the fish to identify whether it's a torpedo or dinner, you know?"

"Maybe there aren't any fish in this river."

"I'm sure there are, but they may all have degrees in clinical psychology."

She scratched a insect bite on her knee. "You're mad, huh? About the minnows and worms."

"No. You were right. Now that I think about it, I wouldn't have wanted to eat a fish that had our minnows or worms in its belly. Bread and water will be adequate, thanks."

"Excuse me. Mind if I make a suggestion?"

Abby's approach was as crafty as Mitch's technique. Once again, Aaron reminded himself that when it came to the female of the species, he was at a disadvantage in more ways than one.

She crouched down between them and unwrapped the paper towel in her hands. Inside were several pieces of cut-up bacon. "When I was your age, Mitch, the old man who lived next door to us always fished with this. Why don't you try it and see if it brings you better luck."

It couldn't hurt and heaven knew it passed Mitch's criterion to qualify as bait: bacon neither wiggled, squirmed nor writhed when poked with a hook. Aaron shot Abby a grateful, if droll, look. "I owe you."

"I know."

"Mitch, bring in your line," Aaron called, pausing midway in cranking the front anchor to check the dark clouds building on the western horizon. "I want to get back on the Mississippi and a few miles farther north before that rain gets here."

"But Uncle Aaron..."

He couldn't believe it. In the last hour she'd caught over a half dozen fish, all of which were hefty enough to keep for a fish fry. "Honey, your arms have to be about worn out."

"They are, but..."

Her voice was drowned out by the sound of the motor as he keyed the ignition. "Abby? Could you help Mitch," he called through the screen door behind him.

"Stop!"

"What?" he yelled back, inching the throttle forward and easing into a wide U-turn.

"*Stop!*"

Aaron killed the engine and ran to the back of the boat. There he found Abby and Mitch standing staring over the railing. "What's wrong?"

"A shark's got my rod," Mitch announced.

Abby stroked the child's ponytail sticking out from behind her hat. "Honey, I don't think there are any sharks in this river."

"Well, it was big enough to pull my rod right out of my hands." She pushed up the bill of the cap to gaze at Aaron. "Can you get it back for me?"

In a way he was flattered. It was reassuring to know his stock had risen to such lofty heights that his youngest niece should think him capable of jumping into this reed-filled feeder river to tangle with who-knew-what variety of animal life, in order to save her property. On the other hand, when it came to exhibitionism, he'd always preferred the intellectual variety over the physical kind. Then he met Abby's gaze.

He cocked his left eyebrow. "What—you, too? Who do I look like, Crocodile Dundee?"

"I yelled for you to stop," she reminded him.

"Sue me. I didn't hear you right away."

"The fish might be a state record. Maybe she'll get her picture in the local paper."

Aaron glanced down into the murky water. "On the other hand, it might be a record-size snapping turtle who's just come off a fast. Or how about a snake?"

"I'm not asking you to go in, Aaron. Look." She pointed toward the motor. "Isn't that her line?"

Aaron did look and spotted it, too. It was caught across the back of the drive-shaft housing, a more welcome sight he couldn't imagine. It still wasn't an easy reach, but preferable to having to do anything foolishly heroic. Ducking between the upper and lower safety railings, he reached for it—but it was beyond his grasp.

"Let me get on the outside and try it," he said, shifting to straddle the railing.

He got close enough to grasp a handful of line and began drawing it in. When he had enough so he could stand, he straddled the rail again for balance and used both hands to draw in the filament. After collecting a few dozen yards of the stuff, up came the rod and reel.

"Where's my fish?" Mitch cried, disappointed.

"Oh, dear," Abby murmured, her attention still focused in the direction of the water.

Aaron looked down again, too, and decided "oh, dear" was right. "I have a feeling there is no fish,

Sunshine. What you caught was a hungry motor. See? The line's wrapped around the propeller,'' he explained, pointing out the problem.

"Phooey,'' she muttered, not convinced.

"It's my fault,'' he acknowledged. "I should have made sure you had it safely in before I started the motor. Abby, would you go to the front and push up on the trim lever. Keep it going until you feel the motor's raised as far as it will go.''

"Are you sure you can reach it?''

He pulled out a small penknife from the back pocket of his jeans. "No, but we can't leave things this way, either. Easy does it, okay? I'd prefer not to go sightseeing in this stuff.''

As she hurried to the front of the boat, Aaron lowered himself back over the side. He watched her give the motor a brief twitch, signaling him that she was about to start. Then up it rose, until only a few inches of propeller remained in the water.

It wasn't the best position, but apparently this was all he was going to get. Again, came the jiggle.

"Thanks!'' he yelled, and leaned out toward the propeller to start working on the mass of line tangled there. Just as he reached it, it began rising again. "Abby!''

He didn't know whether she heard him or not. Either way, it was a moot point. He had balanced too much of his weight on the motor and its abrupt movement caused him to lose his balance. He fell sideways into the algae green water.

When he resurfaced, spit out a mouthful and could see, he glanced up to find Mitch peering over the railing. "Do you see my fish yet, Uncle Aaron?"

As far as martini glasses went, the plastic cocktail cups weren't stylish, let alone traditional, but Abby was pleased to have found them, and the jar of olives, the vermouth and the gin. Normally, Aaron's favorite drink was a bit lethal for her taste, but she felt so badly about his unceremonious dunking, she needed something to soothe her own frayed nerves.

The poor man. He had been such a good sport about the whole thing. It really had been an accident, though. A hornet had shown up out of nowhere and buzzed within an inch of her face. Startled she'd reacted instinctively, by swiping at it; only, in the process, she had taken her hand off the trip switch. When she pushed it again, she'd sent Aaron into his unexpected dive.

Thank goodness he hadn't been seriously hurt. His dignity was somewhat waterlogged, and right now that was her chief concern. Aaron was a proud man, and just when he was doing so well with the girls, this had to happen. All through dinner he had been the source of Mitch's amusement. She'd described his fall again and again. Good sport that he was trying to be, he'd tolerated it. But he deserved better, and she wanted to try to make it up to him.

Once he'd emerged from his dousing, he had gone back up the dock to the small motel next to the bait house. There he'd rented a room and indulged in an extra long hot shower. By the time he'd started back, the storm clouds were too close to attempt moving on, so he made arrangements to tie up to the dock for the night.

Now it was almost dark and the girls had gone off to bed. Aaron had slipped out back to stand under the roof and watch the downpour. Deciding he had been alone too long, Abby picked up both plastic cups and backed out through the screen door.

"Ready or not, I've decided you need my company," she murmured, joining him at the railing. Her bravado was sheer hype, but she took confidence when the surprise in his eyes was replaced by warmth and welcome.

"Is that what I think it is? Where on earth did you get the makings for those?"

"Our quasi-landlord has an extremely interesting secret stash behind his toolbox in the utility closet."

"Bless his black heart," he drawled, accepting one of the cups.

Abby's pulse played leapfrog at the brush of his fingers against hers. He looked so different from the man she was used to dealing with at the courthouse. In his clean tank top and jeans, with his dark hair still damp and slicked back from his shower, he reminded her more of a rebel in an old fifties film than the introspective man who decided men's fates through judicial means.

"Cheers," she murmured, touching her cup to his.

Afterward, Aaron took a sip of his drink. He closed his eyes and sighed. "Mmm...how did you know I wanted one of these?"

"After the teasing you put up with through dinner? You deserve much more." When he lifted an eyebrow in silent comment, she realized the implication of her words and lowered her gaze to her own drink. "You know what I mean. Um...Mitch really did have a good time today."

"She did well, didn't she? No doubt, she'll be reeling in fish even in her sleep." Aaron leaned one shoulder against the wrought-iron support beam. "How about you? Aren't you exhausted, after putting in another long day with the brood?"

"Don't remind me. I'm fast coming to the conclusion that I'm too old to keep up with anyone under twenty-five."

"Listen to you. I'm twelve years older than you are. Think how that makes me feel."

Abby's soft laugh ended with a blissful sigh. She had hoped for this easygoing dialogue. Refocusing on the rain, she murmured, "Isn't it a wonderful evening?"

"If you're into downpours that suggest we're going to be doing forty days and forty nights of this."

"Don't be such a romantic, Aaron." Abby shifted to sit sideways on the first rung of the railing and stretched her free hand to intersect the mini waterfall running off the roof. "I've always loved watching it rain, especially when I'm on water. I like the popping sounds and the patterns of splashes each droplet makes as it hits."

A small frown drew faint lightning bolts between his eyebrows. "Do you know what's just struck me? Outside of your work habits and the technical data about your past, you've never really told me that much about yourself."

"It's not as though we've ever had much time to dwell on such things. Those five-minute rides, when I've accompanied you to a luncheon reception or dinner banquet were usually gobbled up by more important things, like last-minute pointers regarding the focus of your speech or filling you in on the other attending VIPs. As far as I recall, you've never been in a state of mind that's conducive to discussing favorite colors or astrological signs."

"Then it's time we did something about that," he murmured, giving her a faint salute with his cup. "Tell me now. No, first let me guess. Your favorite color is navy blue."

"Violet." This time both of his stark eyebrows shot upward, and Abby laughed to think she'd surprised the man many attorneys complained was unflappable.

"Then why the devil don't you ever wear it? You're always in either navy, gray or black."

"Those are subdued professional colors."

"They're as boring as hell."

"Maybe. But I'm not there to adorn your office, am I?"

"Touché," he murmured, swirling the olive in his drink. He lifted his gaze and studied her with a new interest. "What other surprises are you hiding? What do you do when I'm not overworking you, Abby?"

"When's that?" she teased.

He groaned. "Be kind to me. I've had all the dousing I can handle for one day."

Abby found his wistful, boyish smile as irresistible as his sexier mannerisms. "I like to read...beg my African violets to bloom...write poetry," she confessed.

"Poetry. It seems so—distant from the harsh realities of your job."

"You're gauging it from a point of misconception. Poetry can be as real and harsh as any of those cases that come through your court. And just like those cases, sometimes it does get too sad or difficult to deal with. That's when I put it away and haunt flea markets and estate auctions."

"You collect antiques? Art?"

"Jade."

"I'll be damned...and what's its appeal?"

"I'm not sure. It holds a mystical quality for me."

"Have you ever thought about traveling to the Orient to collect more?"

"I dream of traveling all the time. My boss, however, is an incurable slave driver. I'm lucky if a week of my vacation passes without a call from him asking help for one calamity or another."

Aaron's dark eyes reflected the soft light beaming through the screen door, as he rested one foot on the bottom rung of the railing and leaned toward her. "The beast. Is he really that bad?"

Unable to bear his intense scrutiny, for fear he might see how vulnerable her heart was to him, Abby lowered her eyes. "I always come when you call, don't I?"

"Conscientious, faithful Abby." Aaron placed his index finger under her chin and forced her to meet his gaze. "Lovely Abby." He drew a deep breath and then exhaled somewhat abruptly. "I think it's time."

"For what?"

Instead of answering, he straightened and put his cup on a nearby table. He did the same with hers. When he slipped his arms around her waist and gently drew her to her feet, her heart leaped up to her throat.

"What big eyes you have, Abby," he murmured, drawing her close, closer. "When you tempt a man, you have to be prepared he may yield to that temptation."

She heard him as if she were far away or in a trance. Only instead of feeling free and uninhibited, suddenly all her confidence vanished and she felt chilly, exposed and unsure of herself. That was ridiculous, she knew; after all, she was thirty years old, a divorcee and hardly inexperienced. Yet she couldn't forget how long it had been since she had let anyone kiss her. Brad's treatment of her, of her faith and trust in their marriage, had done a hatchet job on her self-confidence. The mere thought that Aaron might find her inadequate or unexciting filled her with dread.

"You're trembling," he murmured.

"It must be the dampness. It goes straight through me."

"Are you sure? Maybe it's me that's getting to you."

"That would be silly," she replied, her heart beginning to pound so hard she felt it vibrate through her entire body. Even as the words came out, she was trying to decide what to do with her hands. She tried resting them on his upper arms, but that felt awkward. She shifted them to his chest, but the strong beat of his heart and the sensual rise and fall of his solid chest made the contact seem too intimate. "We've known each other for years," she insisted, reminding herself more than him.

"Exactly. We're friends. What would be more natural than for two friends to touch...kiss?"

Abby focused on his mouth and wondered how long she would have to wait. "As a matter of fact, we should be asking ourselves why it took this long."

"Wrong," he muttered against her lips. "We should stop beating around the bush and do something about it." And he did, closing his mouth over hers.

She'd dreamed about this moment so often, for so long, and yet nothing could have prepared her for the absolute wonder of it. He brought the world into focus. Everything became sharper, sweeter, more poignant; the rain suddenly sounded as though the entire river was coming down around them, the honeysuckle on the bank seduced her senses as if she'd swallowed her entire drink in one gulp and every bone in her body was liquefying under his heat.

Aaron kissed with a sureness and precision, as if he had been waiting for this as long as she had. There was no clumsy groping, nose bumping or any of the other innumerable embarrassments that could have turned the moment into a regret. He kissed as if he already knew what she liked, what excited her, what she craved. He kissed as if he understood her. It was so wonderful, she wanted to cry and laugh all at the same time. Most of all, she wanted this moment to last forever.

And his touch...he had wonderful hands. While he seduced her with the most sensually erotic tangling of his tongue, his hands were gentle, sensitive—and was she losing her mind or was he really being *polite?* He stroked her from shoulder to waist—not an inch lower—until, like a masseur, he knew every inch of her better than she knew herself, relaxing her and coaxing her to rest completely against him. But he took it no further.

When he finally lifted his head to let her breathe, it was all she could do to meet his gaze and not sink into a puddle at his feet. He, in turn, stared down at her with the most endearing expressions of bewilderment and desire that, if she wasn't already head-over-heels crazy about the man, would have sent her tumbling.

"Damn," he breathed.

"Could I—" she swallowed to relieve her own dry throat "—could I have a clarification on that? Did you mean, 'Damn, I shouldn't have done that,' or 'Damn, I wish I'd thought of this sooner?'"

His eyes roamed in a slow caress over her face. "It means 'Damn, if we try that again, we're in serious trouble.'"

She didn't know what to say in response to that. She'd already confessed more than, in a saner moment, she would think wise.

"Speechless, Abby? That's not like you."

"At this point, you're something of an unfamiliar entity, yourself."

"Yes, I suppose I am." He smiled, as if the idea appealed to him. "I haven't felt like spending an entire evening pursuing some serious but safe necking in longer than I'd care to remember."

"That's an oxymoron."

"This whole bizarre month has been one. Everything has, except for you . . . the closer I get to you, the more sense it all makes to me." He bent to plant a gentle sucking kiss on her lower lip. "Be glad you have three guardians, my dear. Otherwise, I might be tempted to explore that concept further, not to mention unravel your other mysteries."

"No, you wouldn't," she replied, with a confidence based on happiness rather than common sense.

"What makes you think so?"

"You may be aggressive, but you're not impetuous."

For an instant, he stared at her, his eyes intense and searching. Then, with a whispered oath, he pressed a kiss to the center of her brow. "I've always known you were important to me, Abby, but I'm only beginning to realize how much."

The sudden shift in emotions surprised her and his words touched her deeply. Still, she couldn't quite squelch the brief rush of disappointment. As much as she cherished what he had just said, she couldn't deny it would have been a little more exciting if he'd been wont to show her just how impetuous he could be.

"I've disappointed you."

"What—no. No, of course not."

But she could tell he didn't believe her. For endless seconds he didn't say anything, only looked at her in a way that made her insides go warm and soft and unsteady. Then he was sliding his arms back around her.

"One last time, Abby. Make it long and sweet, sweeter than the scent of that honeysuckle gliding over on the rain."

Abby wrapped her arms around his neck and touched her lips to his. Aaron let her do nothing more, but took control himself. Sweeping her close again, he claimed her lips with his, and lured her into the slow, passionate tempo they'd discovered before, until they were both breathing unsteadily.

Finally, he lifted his head. There was a strained look around his eyes and mouth, and his pulse beat strong at his temples. "You're right," he whispered, his breath hot against her lips. "It wouldn't be a good idea for me to let this get out of hand."

"Maybe it's time for me to check on the girls. They seem to sleep better when I'm with them."

"I'm not surprised. I'll bet you could do wonders for my sleep, too."

She smiled and looked away. "You're being bad."

"I feel like being bad." He spoke, while considering her mouth again. Abruptly, he gave her two more tender kisses on either corner of her lips and then put her at arm's length. "Are you going to dream of me?"

She almost swayed toward him, his words were like a magnet drawing her. "Do you want me to?"

"It would only be fair. What do you think I'll be doing?"

Dreaming of her. What a lovely thought. She picked up her cup, intent on tossing the contents over the side. She no longer needed it.

Aaron's fingers closed over hers. "I may," he said, as though reading her mind.

Her skin tingled, as he took the cup from her. She knew that was the hand she would hold against her heart when she lay in bed unable to sleep. "Good night, then."

"Sweetest dreams, Abby."

She could feel his gaze on her even as she went inside and headed for the bedroom. Never had anyone made her more conscious of her womanliness or made her feel so special. Tonight had changed things. Nothing would ever be quite the same again, and they still had a few more days left on their trip. Though she ached for more of his kisses, she smiled, aware that there would be other tomorrows once they got back to Miami.

Chapter Seven

"Good morning, Delores! And before you ask, yes, I had a wonderful vacation," Abby declared breezing into the outer office of Aaron's chambers. She smiled with pleasure as the other woman's mouth dropped open. "What do you think?" she added, whirling around so that the full skirt of her violet silk dress fanned out around her legs.

"I think you either got home to the news you've won a lottery or you and Judge M. finally had it out and he's in the bottom of the Mississippi River wearing a cement suit," she replied dryly.

No one was ever going to accuse Delores of being a cheerleader, and she'd long had a insider's view of Abby's unique relationship with Aaron. Still, Abby liked the middle-aged woman's droll wit, and she knew it was no reflection of her dedication to her job and their boss. Shaking her head in response to either suggestion, Abby set her purse and leather briefcase on the edge of Delores's desk and passed over the gift-wrapped package she'd been carrying under her other arm. "This is a belated birthday present."

"Oh, goody...give it here." Delores wasted no time on insincere hesitation; she snatched the gift and started ripping off the lace ribbon and floral tissue paper. "No matter what it is, it has to be better than what Marty gave me."

"What's he done, now?" Abby asked, knowing how Delores loved to embellish on the stories she told about her spouse, though the woman was truly crazy about the man.

"The big lug bought me a lawn mower for my birthday. He's lucky I haven't given him a haircut with it. Once I saw it, I said I'd never accept a present again, but—oh!" She gazed with wonder at her gift. "You sure do know how to tempt a girl. My, will you look at this."

Upon their return to New Orleans, Abby had found an original painting of a southern plantation at an arts-and-crafts fair. It was a scene complete with Spanish moss-draped trees, framing a house with a beautifully landscaped yard and pond. She knew it was perfect for the feisty woman who was really a romantic at heart. "I hope you like it."

"Like it? I love it!" Beneath her pageboy hairdo, Delores's basset-hound face took on a determined expression. "And I know exactly where this is going— I don't care how much Marty complains. I've told him time and time again that bull-on-velvet thing over the couch isn't going to appreciate in value. Now I can show him what real art's supposed to look like. Well, thanks, honey. I can't tell you how touched I am."

"The girls helped me choose it."

"Did they? That makes it all the more special," she said, rising to place the picture on top of a filing cabinet where she could view it from her seat. "How are those cuties? Did they have a good time?"

"Eventually." Abby spent the next few moments filling her in on the highlights of their trip. "By the end, they came around."

Delores drew her bifocals farther down her nose and gave Abby another thorough once-over. "I'd say everything turned out to everyone's satisfaction. Nice dress."

"Thank you. I decided a little more color around here wouldn't hurt."

"New hairdo, too."

Abby touched the soft waves held back from her face by two tortoiseshell combs. She'd had to get up an hour earlier to achieve this look. "You don't think it's too much?"

"Much? No. Surprising? We're talking maybe a 7.5 on the Richter scale. So what can I expect from our fearless leader? I gotta tell you, honey, if he tramps in here looking anything other than his conservative self, I'm going have to go home and get my video camera to save all this for posterity."

Abby was about to remark on that, but the entry door burst open with a swooshing sound and along with a blast of colder refrigerated air came Aaron. He looked tanned and fit in a summer gray suit and—furious. Without giving Abby or Delores a glance, he strode straight for the door to his chambers.

"Delores, hold all calls, and I mean all of them. Syd Wendell is right behind me. Let him and his so-called assistants in, then bolt the door if you have to, but keep everyone else out. I'm not making any comments to the press. You'll also have to phone and cancel my luncheon appointment. Abby, in my office *now*."

She stared as he disappeared around the door.

"Whew," Delores whispered. "Something's hit the fan."

But did he have to react like this? Abby couldn't stop the hurt she felt at being treated so briskly, not to mention being ignored as though she'd been part of the furniture.

"Abby!"

His roar snapped her out of her self-pity and propelled her after him. Shooting Delores a speaking glance and receiving a quick shrug in return, she followed him inside, shutting the door behind her.

He was already in his office and shedding his jacket in a way that threatened to do some serious damage to the seams. Abby reached for it, only to watch Aaron walk past her. In a burst of temper, he threw it onto his chair and stalked to his closet.

"Find Feldman. He should already be on his way down here," he added checking his watch. "Tell him—"

"Aaron what's wrong?" Abby injected, trying to keep her own agitation out of her voice.

"For crying out loud, will you do as you're told? All hell's broken loose on the Mantia case, and I want to speak to his attorney. Do you understand?"

There was barely time to wince at the biting rebuke, before Syd Wendell came in followed by his number two man, Patterson, and the young D.A. who'd relieved him on the case, Jeffrey Childs. While both of the younger men looked as though they'd already been through the ringer, the three of them shared expressions that clearly stated they would rather have walked out of a 747 over the Atlantic Ocean without a parachute than be where they were now.

"Ah, gentlemen," Aaron said, cordiality dripping with sarcasm. "How good of you to accept my invitation. I thought perhaps you'd be tied up busily destroying the rest of your cases."

The grim-faced district attorney drew a deep breath. "Aaron, I know this looks bad, but getting upset isn't going—"

"Looks bad? It is bad, Syd," Aaron shot back. He jerked open his closet door and yanked out his robe, which he slipped on with the energy of someone who could easily punch holes into the plastered walls. "You had a cut-and-dried case. Santos Mantia is a nickel-and-dime criminal, who's been costing the taxpayer thousands of dollars every year breezing in and out of this courthouse like a damned air-freight courier. Now, when you have him ready to do life, *life*, what do your people do? Lose critical evidence."

"Aaron, the gun had just gone through ballistics and somehow it got misplaced between there and the evidence room," Syd Wendell tried to explain. "I'm sure it'll show up."

"In the next fifteen minutes? Because that's when we're going to trial, gentlemen."

"If we could have a little more time..."

"I can give you an hour. No more."

Patterson and Childs, Abby noted, went from gray to green. Their eyes never rose above the knot of Aaron's black, red and silver tie.

"I was hoping for something more like a day or two," the district attorney replied, his own coloring unhealthy.

"To do what? Find a poor sucker to take the blame for your mutual sloppiness? One hour, Syd, then we open. In the meantime, may I suggest you train Childs here in some fast footwork, because I guarantee you the defense will take this opportunity to ask for great latitude in answering your questions... and I'm going to have no option but to give it to him."

The trio left without another word. Aaron jerked off his robe and flung it on the couch. When he turned back around, he frowned slightly, as if noticing Abby for the first time.

"Did you get Feldman?"

"N-no. I haven't even tried yet. Aaron, don't you think you're being rather—"

"Damnation, Abby, either find Feldman or hire me someone who can follow orders, all right?"

Not wanting to hear any more, she raced from his office.

* * *

She hated tears. Even as a child when she'd been pushed off a school bus and broke her arm, she'd fought hard not to cry. Crying never solved anything; it hadn't made her threadbare clothes look like her schoolmates' when she'd been a child, and it didn't make her parents' ramshackle house in South Carolina look any different than what it was. All tears did was redden and swell your eyes and give you the sniffles, leaving you not only feeling miserable but looking worse.

She dug into her pocket for the last of her tissues and blew her nose. To think she'd believed things had changed. How could he snap at her like that? He had treated her as if she were the one responsible for that lost gun. Worse, he had treated her as if the last two weeks hadn't happened. Whatever they'd shared had obviously meant more to her than it did to him.

Just thinking of the days and special moments that had followed their first kisses made her heart ache. He had been so kind to her after that, so thoughtful and sweet, rarely allowing himself to be alone with her. She'd believed it was because he thought he couldn't trust himself; now she wondered. Had it all been meaningless, a game? Had any of those intimate moments, those long, searching kisses meant anything?

Just as she tossed the tissues into the trash bin, the bathroom door swung open. Before she could seek cover inside one of the cubicles, she heard Delores's New York accent.

"Relax, hon, it's only me."

Relieved, Abby peeked around the corner. "Sorry. I know I've been in here forever. I'll be back to the office in a minute. Is he looking for me?"

"No. Court's still in session. From the sound of things he's teaching everyone a lesson in there. My guess is you've already learned yours for the day."

Abby's laugh held no humor. She abandoned her hiding spot and joined her workmate. "For a lifetime." A glance into the mirror running the length of the sinks had her moaning. "I need a pair of sunglasses."

"Honey, you need a momma. Since yours has passed on and I'm practically the oldest thing here to qualify, it looks like I'm elected. You want to talk now or go back to my desk?"

The thought of anyone, *Aaron*, walking in on them, had Abby shaking with dread. "No, I can't go back there yet. What if he came in?"

"Then he'd see a woman whose heart is breaking because he's behaved like an insensitive jerk. It sounds like a smart move to me."

"Oh, Delores." Abby sniffed ignoring the suggestion. "I think I've made the biggest mistake."

The shorter, wiry woman whipped a paper towel from the dispenser and wet it with cool water. "You aren't the first and you won't be the last, honey. Here, this rough stuff may give you wrinkles, but the cool water will reduce the swelling. Dab it under your eyes and tell me all about it. That trip did more than smooth things out between him and those kids, didn't it?"

Though, up to this moment, Abby had been keeping her feelings about Aaron a secret, she told Delores almost everything. The only things she couldn't bring herself to share were those moments when she and Aaron were alone; the moments just before the girls rose in the morning or after they went to bed at night, when Aaron would seek her out and they would talk, stare at one another, kiss. Each episode edged them closer and closer toward an inevitable choice.

"You're in love with him."

Abby forced the memories back and blinked at her workmate. "Can I plead the Fifth on that?"

Shrugging, Delores took the paper towel from her and rinsed it with fresh, cooler water. "You can do whatever you want, but it won't change the obvious. Now hold that to your forehead." She clucked sympathetically. "You sure do pick them, honey."

"Aaron's a wonderful judge," Abby declared, following an immediate instinct to come to his defense.

"Sure. He's also handsome as sin, and as far as I know he's never kicked a puppy. But when it comes to women and consideration of their needs and feelings, the man's got the instincts of a blind samurai in a crystal shop. He's cutting your heart out. Why aren't you mad? Angry. Grrr," Delores said, curling her fingers into claws and pretending to snarl. "Why are you letting him do this to you?"

It was bad enough to once again allow herself to be humiliated by a man she loved, but to have her behavior criticized by a friend right afterward was one offense too many. Abby flung the water-soaked paper towel into the waste receptacle and cried, "Can't I be allowed to get over the hurt first?"

Delores merely smiled and, crossing her arms, she leaned back against the tile wall.

Frustration boiled in Abby. "You needn't look so pleased with yourself. I'm angry. Fine! Are you satisfied?"

"Nope. But we'll get there. The idea, though, is to please you. Sooner or later you're going to have to face him. What are you going to say when you do? Now, admittedly, I may not have been here from the beginning of your relationship, but even when I joined on, I could see the patterns you were creating between between your ex and Aaron."

Despite the sting Abby felt at being criticized, she had to ask. "What do you mean?"

"You know. You've allowed yourself to become a doormat. First you supported Brad's career and adjusted your entire life around his schedule and his needs. You even accepted his bad habits, because you thought that's what a good wife does. Now you're doing the same thing to Aaron, and look what's happened."

"There's no comparison. Aaron's my boss. How could I be giving him the same signals?"

Delores rolled her eyes. "You're in love with him. Only, to you, that seems to come with the word 'unconditional' before it. It's the biggest mistake a woman can allow to happen. He's taking you for granted, now. You've become an extra rib to him, an office wife. The trouble is, you've not getting any of the benefits."

"I'm not looking for 'benefits,'" Abby scoffed.

"You still don't get it. What I mean is, when was the last time he did something nice for you?"

"He does nice things for me all the time. The one thing you can't take away from Aaron is that he's a gentleman."

"I'm not talking about opening doors."

"When we work overtime, or anything, he always pays for my meals or the taxi to get me home."

"That goes on his expense account, honey. When was the last time he sent you flowers? Remember last secretaries' day? You both gave me flowers. When's it your turn to be appreciated—and as a *woman*, not just an employee?"

Abby didn't want to think of Delores as being right, but with every second that passed the truth became more evident. And she had no one to blame but herself. That did make her angry. She'd paid a tremendous price to learn her lesson the first time with Brad; how could she have let herself fall into the same mistake again?

She turned to face her reflection. It cost her, not to burst into tears at the hurt and devastation she saw there. She turned on the water taps. "I need a minute to wash my face and redo my makeup. Then I'll be back inside."

Her low, emotionless tone must have upset her friend, because Delores touched her shoulder. "Are you okay? Maybe I shouldn't have come down so hard on you. Marty's warned me that I've got the tact of a wrecking ball."

"No, you said exactly what I need to hear," Abby told her, though she continued to stare at her own reflection. "I've made a career out of giving and giving, and now the reservoir is empty. It's time to do something about that.''

Aaron was drained and disappointed when he exited the courtroom and returned to his chambers. The only satisfaction he could take was that he'd made his feelings about the Mantia case clear: sloppiness would not be tolerated in his court. There was no excuse for putting a murderer back on the street, and the district attorney's office—as well as the police department—would think twice before they ever came to him with excuses again.

The clock on his credenza indicated that it was past one. He shrugged out of his robe and hung it in the closet. His stomach growled, reminding him the bite of toast he'd had for breakfast was long gone. He had overslept and there hadn't been one of Abby's wonderful meals waiting for him after he'd showered and shaved.

Thinking of Abby, he glanced down through the narrow hall separating their offices. It was so quiet, he wondered if she was out for lunch herself. It wouldn't be like her; she always waited to see if he wanted her to bring something back for him. Then, again, he could expect her to wait only so long.

"Abby?"

There was a slight shuffling sound, papers being moved. Satisfied, he went to his desk to begin sorting through his phone messages and mail. After two weeks' absence, it was going to take a while to work through it.

"Yes?"

He glanced up at her, ready to give her a wry smile. He'd been so busy this morning, they hadn't had a chance to say hello or catch up on how each of them had spent what was left of the weekend. But the moment he saw her, his eyes widened.

He didn't know where to look first. Her dress was violet... *violet;* recalling what she'd said about the color, he thought how lovely she looked in it. It made her skin seem translucent, and added intriguing shadows to her indigo blue eyes. And her hair; she had never worn it down and curled so that it tumbled around her shoulders like a pale gold cloud. How it tempted him to go to her and run his fingers through it.

"Wow... did you have that on when I came in today?"

It wasn't, he realized, the wisest thing he could have said. Her mouth, already unsmiling, turned tight-lipped and grim, and the expression in her eyes wasn't reassuring, either.

He grimaced, and gestured to encompass the room. "Things here were crazy this morning. I'm sorry for not noticing. You look wonderful."

"Did you need something in particular?"

She was annoyed all right. Aaron rubbed the back of his neck and offered a sheepish smile. "What can I say to make things right?"

"I'm on my way to lunch. I see you've already located your mail and messages. There isn't anything else pending that's dire, so I'm going to run some errands. I'll be late getting back, but Delores said she'd cover for me."

As she turned to leave, Aaron hurried around his desk and grabbed her arm. "Hey, easy does it." The dress was silk. He liked the feel of it against her skin and shifted both hands to her shoulders, massaging them. "I think we should talk. I know you're hurt that I didn't notice how great you looked when—"

"That's the least of my complaints."

It was? Aaron shook his head, at a loss as to what to say. "Then what did I do wrong?"

Abby swung around and stared at him. "You actually don't know, do you?" she said at last. "You haven't a clue."

He tried to find one. He replayed the morning's events through his mind once again; but all he came up with was that he'd been madder than hell at Syd Wendell and his people because, unless a miracle happened, a murderer was going to be a free man, perhaps as early as this time tomorrow.

"Maybe I was too hard on Syd and his boys, when I chewed them out this morning, but—"

"You know what hurts more than anything, Aaron?" Abby injected, moving a step back to counter his step forward. "It's the fact that you don't recall what else you did. You were rude, disrespectful and unfair to me this morning. To *me*."

"I was?" He replayed the scene again, but with little more success. "All I remember is that I asked you to find Feldman for me. Surely you agree that Mantia's counsel had a right to know the status of things before we opened?"

"You didn't ask, you ordered," Abby snapped. "And when I didn't react fast enough to suit you, you became as sarcastic to me as you were to District Attorney Wendell and his assistants. That was hard to take, Aaron. But what made it unbelievable was that it happened barely two days after we returned from our trip, where you'd pretended to be an entirely different person.''

"Pretended?" He still felt as if she had to be talking about someone else. Only the tears reddening her eyes—eyes, he now realized, that were already red and slightly swollen, underlining how serious she was. "Abby, the only thing I wasn't doing was pretending."

"Save it. I've done my share of listening to empty declarations or anything else. My God," she cried, her voice cracking. "To think I thought you were different. What a fool I was. If anything, your style is smoother, because you know how to get your money's worth. Flatter a female enough and she'll do anything for you, even follow you up the Mississippi and baby-sit your nieces. Delores, was right, I am a doormat."

Aaron stiffened. "I did not use you. Admittedly, at first my motives were based primarily on need. Sure, I asked you along because I *trusted* you, what was wrong with that? Furthermore, I was right to. The girls were talking about you even as they boarded their plane home."

"I see, so the moonlight romancing was my tip for services rendered."

"Is that how you see it?" he asked, feeling something go still inside him.

"What am I supposed to think, when you behave like you did this morning?"

"I don't remember how I acted this morning!"

His declaration reverberated through the room. For several seconds silence reigned, until Abby shook her head and began to turn to leave again.

"What about us?" he demanded, following her.

"There is no us, Aaron."

"The hell there isn't. I held you." He did again, swinging her around and into his arms. "Kissed you." He lowered his head seeking her lips.

Abby fought him like a person fighting drowning in a flood. "Let me go," she muttered, averting her head and pushing at his chest. "Let . . . me . . . go."

A certain note in her voice reached him, because suddenly he let go and she stumbled backward, steadying herself against the doorjamb.

"There is no us," she said again. "At one time I hoped there would be. You want a good laugh? I've had a crush on you forever, and I thought that if I could just make you notice me outside my work, that you'd realize . . . Never mind," she muttered, bowing her head. "The important thing is that I came to my senses in time."

Aaron ignored the coldness that was creeping into his soul, and forced himself to ask, "Would you care to expand on that?"

"You're a wonderful judge, Aaron, and if you don't work yourself into a rut and lose contact again, you're going to be a great uncle. But you don't know the first thing about women or how to begin to make one happy."

Pride stung, he lifted his chin. "I haven't had many complaints—until now."

"No, but, then, you also have a talent for dating women who know the score. They know your work does and always will come first and that romance is a tangible thing with you...a bracelet, flowers, an expensive dinner at a popular restaurant, and there ends your conscience. I realize, now, that the man I cared about would have to give me more."

"Like?"

"His time. His complete attention, even if it's just for a walk in the country or sharing a bowl of popcorn while watching a movie. That's a price you'd find too high to pay, Aaron, no matter what lip service you paid the idea before. Little things and real emotional intimacy aren't in the forefront of your vocabulary or in your budget."

"And what makes you the sudden expert on reliable men?"

He only said it out of hurt and his own anger, but Aaron knew he'd made a giant error as soon as he spoke. He regretted the words twice as much, when he saw the effect they had on Abby. The blood drained from her face and he knew he would carry the memory of the pain in her eyes for many a sleepless night to come.

When she spun around and headed for her own office, he went after her. "I didn't mean it," he said, grasping her arm again.

She shrugged him off.

"Abby, it was said in a moment of—of frustration. Don't you ever react without thinking?"

"I'm about to." Picking up her purse, she started for the door. Aaron blocked her way. "Let me go," she demanded.

"If you'll just let me explain . . ."

"Aaron, if you don't let me go this instant, I swear I'll quit here and now, and not even give you the courtesy of two weeks notice."

They were at the door, and he froze. For a moment, they stared at one another, anger, disbelief and a myriad of other emotions all in one knot. Then, Abby jerked the door open and left.

Aaron stood there and watched, barely aware of Delores sitting at her desk eyeing him calmly. "Hold all calls," he managed, when the exit door slammed behind Abby.

"That should solve all your problems," Delores drawled.

Not at all pleased with what he was tempted to say in response to that, Aaron shut his own door.

Chapter Eight

Abby never did come back that afternoon. Around four, Delores rang Aaron in his office and informed him she'd called in complaining of feeling ill and that she had decided to go straight home. Shortly afterward he left, himself.

He played with the idea of going to her place. A part of him felt she didn't have a right to say the things she'd said, without giving him an opportunity for a rebuttal. After some deliberation, however, he acknowledged that maybe he was better off that way. Maybe stating his own case or whatever it was he had planned to do—and right now he wasn't sure—might just as easily make things worse.

The early hour was a benefit; traffic was light all the way to his house. The way his mind wandered, his sedan could have driven itself to the one-storied Spanish-style brick structure. He only realized he was home, when he pulled under the electrically monitored garage door and found himself sitting in the dark garage with the engine idling. He shut off the car, collected his briefcase and the personal mail he'd picked up from the estate's security office and went inside.

The house was silent. After a month of living with three energetic girls, that seemed unnatural. In the kitchen, he found the usual note from Mrs. Kaminski. He couldn't even chuckle over her wry comments about it taking her a mere two hours to get the fingerprints off the smoked-glass cabinet doors. As he considered the honey-toned paneling and the blue-tiled counters, along with the stainless-steel fixtures, he found it almost impossible to think that anything in the past month had actually happened. All signs of the girls' visit were gone, and Abby would definitely not be dropping by to check on him. He was a full-fledged bachelor again. Alone. It filled him with a loneliness that had him reaching for the mail to shut off his mind.

It didn't sink in until he'd finished flipping through it, that he was looking for a letter from the girls. It was impossible for there to be one, since he'd only put them on a plane yesterday. Besides, just because they promised to write, didn't mean they would. They were young and anxious to be home again with their parents. They had other things on their minds. He would be forgotten. Tossing the mail on the counter, he went to the living room to the bar and poured himself a drink.

He had always enjoyed his house; from the moment he'd first walked through it with the real-estate agent six years ago, he'd felt comfortable here. It was more than appreciating the rich wood paneling and accents or the custom tile floors the original owner had designed to draw the living room, kitchen and foyer together; every room held the same qualities of uniqueness and welcome.

But, today, even the bright sunlight beaming down through the dual sunlights couldn't warm him. In fact, he felt cold.

He unlocked the sliding-glass door and stepped out on the back deck, into heat and humidity. It engulfed him like a cocoon, but it was a nostalgic, desirable assault. He slid off his suit jacket, laid it over a wrought-iron chair and wrenched his tie loose. Better, he thought, taking a sip of his watered-down Scotch. His day had been spent in far too much refrigerated air.

The sun wasn't low enough to cast its usual sheen of molten gold on the canal, but the water glistened with a different light, like a polished black pearl. Drawn to it, Aaron descended the wood-and-slate stairs, rounded his pool and crossed the lawn.

When he'd first moved here, he'd planted a cypress tree near his private dock; now he paused and leaned against it, while observing the ripples of water splashing against the dock. There was no traffic at the moment. At this hour, his neighbors were either still at work, lingering over a late lunch or catching an afternoon nap before starting the evening round of dinner parties. He listened to this insular quiet; it made him think, not of the bad times, the memories of moments gone sour, but of the times on the boat when the girls, exhausted from swimming, would take a nap and he and Abby sit and watch the world drift by.

Abby. Was the lessening of one haunting only going to be replaced with another? All he had to do was think of her and his insides tied into knots all over again. Where was she? What was she doing? Was she all right? Throughout the afternoon, he had replayed their conversation again and again in his mind, and he still couldn't believe she'd said some of the things she did.

That accusation about his not understanding women stung the most. Of course, he understood them... didn't he? Adrienne, for example, had never complained. Then, again, Abby was right; Adrienne had known the score from the beginning. All right, then before her there had been... there had been... damn. Either he was going senile or he'd had fewer memorable relationships than he'd believed. But did that make him insensitive? A boor?

Romance. Now there she was wrong. He had found it with Abby. It had to have been romance, because there certainly hadn't been anything special about that damned boat to prompt what had evolved between them. Lord, even in retrospect he couldn't believe things had turned out the way they did. Granted, it hadn't been what he would label a perfect trip, but there had been moments—all of them with Abby— when he'd never felt more alive. And having shared that with him, how could she try to insist there was nothing between them?

Aaron took a long sip of his drink and sought answers. If only he'd kept better control of his temper this morning with the Mantia case. Usually, he wasn't so quick on the trigger, but when he'd seen his standards were going to be compromised...

He had to face it; he blew it, and Abby had paid the ultimate price. How could he have hurt her like that?

She was threatening to quit. The thought that she was capable of it made him heartsick—not because he would be losing a damned good assistant, but because it would mean her intention was never to see him again. He couldn't let it happen. But what to do? What to do...?

Gardening around the house had always helped clear her head when she was having problems, but repotting African violets in her apartment didn't seem to be doing the trick. Abby didn't let that stop her, however; she figured that since she already had the dirt under her fingernails, she might as well finish the job. What made it difficult, was stopping periodically to blow her nose.

Damn the man—he wasn't worth her tears. Abby took the Red Sparkler she'd found at the supermarket—where she'd stopped because she was out of aspirin—from its plastic container and set it into a clay pot. She would show him. With her skills and experience, not to mention the contacts she'd made over the years, there were undoubtedly numerous people who would jump at the chance to hire her out from under Aaron. She could even go back to school and finish getting her law degree. It wasn't something she'd been aspiring to do, but it was an option. At this stage of her life, options took on more importance, didn't they? She was, after all, thirty and single. While her biological clock hadn't yet started ticking, it wasn't looking like she was going to have anything besides work on her hands for a while to come.

The problem was, she didn't want to get her degree, and she didn't give a heck about options, either. She wanted Aaron—only not the Aaron she'd met this morning. Her eyes stung anew just remembering that. Nor did she want the blind fool who still couldn't see what was in front of his eyes.

As the tears spilled over her lashes, Abby wiped them away with the back of her hand. Wet potting soil fell off the tablespoon she was using, bounced off the newspaper she'd spread out to work on and landed on her champagne-colored carpet.

Perfect, she thought, exhaling her exasperation. She'd been dropping things all afternoon. First she had splattered a ripe tomato in the supermarket, then she had dropped her dry cleaning in the parking lot...all she needed now was for this stuff to stain her rug.

Carefully picking up the clumps, she tossed them back onto the newspaper. Then she continued filling in more dirt around the newly potted plant.

There, she thought, with a satisfied nod; a new addition to her collection. She eyed the profusion of plants and then her new acquisition with appreciation. She might have no luck with men, but at least she had a talent for making things grow and bloom. A knock at the door, however, almost had her dropping everything and making a bigger mess.

Now what? she thought, scowling, as she gingerly set down her new plant. She wasn't in the mood for company, regardless of whether it was someone selling something or one of her neighbors. Maybe if she was quiet, they would go away.

But they didn't. After a few seconds, they knocked again, this time harder.

Some people didn't know how to take a hint. Abby sniffed again, rubbed the tip of her nose and, unwinding herself from her lotus-like position on the carpet, stood. Tiptoeing to the door, she peered through the security hole.

Aaron. Her heart lurched painfully in her chest. What was he doing here? Oh, Lord...she couldn't open the door, she looked a mess. Her eyes were redder than before, and the salmon pink terry-cloth playsuit she was wearing had been washed to near colorlessness.

"Abby? I know you're in there," he said, his voice urgent but low. "I can see your car."

Well, maybe I'm out on a date. Has that crossed your mind? Abby fumed, wishing she could ask that out loud. Of course, considering what he'd said to her earlier today, her dating was the last thing he would think of.

"I'm not leaving until you answer. I just need to know you're all right."

That was all she needed, him planting himself out there like an ornamental bush. She only happened to have the two nosiest neighbors in all of Miami living on either side of her, and what Mrs. Newberry missed, Mrs. Lowenstein usually filled her in on. The neighborhood didn't need a security guard, with those two around.

Abby gave in. As she went to the door, her gaze fell on the side table bearing her purse, keys and sunglasses. Sunglasses! Snatching them up, she put them on and then unbolted the door. Potting soil was soon smeared over brass. Ugh, she thought, why hadn't she taken a moment to wipe off her hands first? More annoyed than ever, she jerked open the door.

He filled her doorway—an illusion, she promptly told herself, brought on because she was barefoot and therefore at a disadvantage. She was also determined to ignore the fact that he was even more handsome than usual. He had taken off his jacket, his tie was gone, and his white dress shirt was unbuttoned at the throat and the sleeves were rolled up to expose his darkly tanned arms. But determined though she was, she still gulped.

Don't start getting soft now, she warned herself. *So what if he looks almost haggard and drawn, or if his eyes are shadowed, haunted.* It probably had nothing to do with her; he probably had experienced more problems after hearing initial arguments in the Mantia case. Served him right, considering what he'd done to her.

"Yes?" The question didn't come out as strong as she'd hoped, but at least it sounded clipped.

He offered her a crooked smile, which soon waned when she refused to return it. "Hi. I don't suppose you'd buy the story that I was in the neighborhood?"

"The North Pole would grow palm trees first. What do you want, Aaron? As you can see, I'm busy."

"Uh—yes." His gaze dropped to her hands, which she'd displayed, palms up to prove her point. He glanced around her, trying to see inside. "I didn't know you have a garden. Is it out back?"

In response, she crossed her arms beneath her breasts. She wasn't any more inclined to make small talk than she was willing to make this easy on him.

When she didn't reply, Aaron hung his head and sighed. "Okay. I don't blame you. But I just needed to know you were all right."

"I'm fine. Terrific, as a matter of fact," she added, because her voice sounded congested and weepy, even to her own ears. "And I'm in the middle of something, so..."

As she began to shut the door, he placed his hand on the outside and pushed back. "Wait. Here." He thrust what looked to be a cake box at her.

Abby had been trying not to notice the box. Now she stared down at it with renewed suspicion. It was tied shut with a shiny green elastic ribbon and bore a gold label identifying its source as the gourmet delicatessen a few miles from here. Her ire rose. If the man thought she was going to invite him inside, just because he had brought along his own hot-to-go dinner, she had a surprise for him.

"I was worried that you wouldn't take care of yourself. You always take care of others and forget yourself, Abby," he said quietly. "And I knew you'd be in no frame of mind to cook."

Well, at least he'd gotten that right. Still, there was the principle of the matter to consider. "I can't accept this."

"There are no strings attached."

"That'll be the day."

"All right, maybe just a small one."

"I rest my case," she drawled, offering the box back to him.

Instead of taking it, he ran a hand through his hair. "Abby, I'm falling fast here. Will you at least let me come in? Hear me out?"

"No."

"Then I'll say what I have to say here. By the way, are you aware that your neighbor on my left has her door cracked and she's eavesdropping?"

Mrs. Lowenstein. Abby groaned inwardly. Might her late mother-in-law—a woman to be feared, from the stories Magda had shared about her—come back and haunt her. Feeling as though some invisible hand was once again turning the tables of good fortune on her, she stepped back and allowed Aaron into her apartment.

If she had noticed the slightest smile on his face, she would have tossed his gourmet peace offering at him and ordered him back out. But he only looked around, his hands thrust into his pockets, looking unbelievably sexy for a man who was trying to be humble.

What did he see, she wondered glancing around herself. The apartment was a shoe box compared to his house, though she liked the layout well enough. A kitchen, dinette and living room on the ground floor and the large bedroom and bath upstairs were all there was. But the colors were appealing; champagne and teal, elegant to the eye and soothing on the nerves. Usually, she amended, feeling his gaze return to her and grow more intense.

"Nice," he murmured, though he was taking in her attire, her bare legs and her feet.

She curled her toes into the thick pile, wanting to hang on to reality any way she could. "I like it."

"Even this," he added, running a finger down her nose before she could back out of his reach. He held it up to indicate a smudge of dirt.

Abby almost made the matter worse by nearly touching her fingers to her nose again. Catching herself in the last moment, she set the box on the coffee table and hurried over to the kitchen bar, where she grabbed a napkin out of its holder. She gave a swipe to her nose and then rubbed her hands.

"All right, you're in," she said, determined to salvage her dignity. "Now please say what you came to say and then leave."

"Do fluorescent lights bother you?"

"Pardon?"

"The sunglasses. I've never noticed the lights bothering you at work. Do they? Or were you working out back, as well as in here?"

He knew perfectly well why she had the glasses on, and he wasn't going to embarrass her into admitting it, either. Abby pushed the rims back up her nose and pointed to the box. "You can take that with you on your way out."

"No, I can't. The main course is a Cornish hen, and you know, after all the banquets I attend, that if I never see any variety of fowl on my plate again, it'll be too soon. I was hoping you'd open the bottle of chardonnay, though. I'd take a glass of that."

The man had nerve, she would give him that. She was tempted to offer him the whole bottle—over his head. On the other hand, if he was determined to stay—and it appeared he was—then she needed something to bolster her own nerves.

Without further comment, she snatched up the box and stalked to the kitchen.

"This is impressive," he called after her. "When you said African violets, I had no idea you were talking about a veritable rain forest."

Abby knew he was referring to the two bakers' racks she had converted into multileveled light gardens, featuring dozens and dozens of plantings and starters from favorite species. She was proud of her accomplishment, and it was on the tip of her tongue to tell him how she practically kept the entire complex in new plants. But she caught herself in time and, remaining silent, she opened and poured the already chilled wine.

The other contents in the box looked equally impressive; besides the hen there were sourdough rolls, a cold pasta salad and some decadently rich-looking chocolate dessert she didn't dare take too close a peek at. Not caring if it was cheating or not, Abby took a long sip of her wine and refilled the glass before carrying both to the living room.

"You've got an impressive collection of jade, too," Aaron said, turning from the corner curio cabinet. "But you never told me that you liked elephants."

"You never asked."

"What's the attraction?"

"They never forget, either."

Aaron swallowed almost half his wine in one gulp. They were both doing it a disservice, Abby thought, willing to admit he did know his wines. The problem was she didn't know how to let go of her fear and her expectation that he would hurt her again.

"I'm trying to find the right words, Abby."

She couldn't bring herself to look at him, instead focusing on the deep gold color of her wine, which was accented by the curio cabinet's light. "I know," she acknowledged. "But you'll understand if I remind you I'm feeling a bit gun shy."

"Would you like to know how I felt when you didn't come back to the office?"

"A result of missing your lunch, no doubt. Your blood sugar was probably low."

"I felt lousy, and it had nothing to do with my blood-sugar level. In fact, I left early, too, only when I got home, I felt worse instead of better."

"Guilt."

"True," he murmured, inclining his head. "And a lot of other things. So I did the only thing I could think of to do."

"I don't want to hear empty rhetoric, Aaron," Abby said, afraid she might lose control over her tentative calm again, if he started. "Don't forget I've heard every excuse in the book. I feel underappreciated and—and used."

He nodded. "That's why I'm here. I want us to try again, Abby. But I also want there to be a clear understanding between us."

Her heart pounding, Abby asked, "And what's that?"

He took a step toward her, his gaze tender but direct. "I'm not Brad. If I make a mistake—and it appears I have the ability to make some whoppers—I want to be judged on my error alone. I don't want to pay for his, as well."

Abby gripped her drink tighter. She had always known he had a talent for getting to the core of things, but this time he'd outdone himself. "For a man who came to mend fences, you certainly have a unique way of going about it."

"I know, but we might as well get all our problematic issues dealt with right from the beginning."

"Why?"

"Because, one way or another, you're going to have to deal with me being in your life."

"I could always quit my job," she reminded him stubbornly.

"You could, and I imagine one day you will." Very calmly, he set his glass down and then carefully took hold of her shoulders. "But when you do, it'll be for reasons other than being hurt and angry," he said, lowering his head toward hers. "Because I'm not going to do that to you again."

She did not want him this close, where he could feel how her body betrayed its vulnerability to him, and she certainly didn't want him to kiss her. But he did.

The pressure of his lips against hers was undemanding, yet firm, and for all her silent resistance, Abby's blood immediately raced through her body with messages of joy and desire. How could she ever hope to protect her tender heart, when, at his first probe, she parted her lips to him letting him take what he would from her?

He made her ache and need. Behind her closed lids, she could see them sinking gracefully to the carpet,

Aaron leaning over her, his chest heaving with restrained longing. He would spread slow kisses down her throat and across her shoulders until he came to the elastic top of her playsuit. And then ...

"Holy Mississippi..." Aaron rasped, breaking their kiss to take a deep breath. "Honey, do you realize you just poured a half glass of wine down the front of my shirt?"

Abby blinked. They weren't on the carpet, but Aaron's chest was indeed heaving; and the front of his shirt was, indeed, plastered to his chest. When he set her at arm's distance and released her, she couldn't quite hold back a sound of regret. Luckily, he misinterpreted it.

"It doesn't matter. Things were about to get out of hand again, anyway." He shot her a rueful smile. "It seems they always do between us. You know if you get any less inhibited at kissing, I'm going to have to start carrying around a fire extinguisher with me." Brushing the front of his shirt, he added, "I wanted to say more, but I'd better get out of here. It would seem my system's had enough stimulus for one evening."

Abby didn't trust herself to reply. Instead, she gulped down what was left of her wine.

Leaning over to give her a hard parting kiss, Aaron went to the door. "I'll see you tomorrow."

Tell him you might not be in. Tell him you've booked an around-the-world cruise and that you'll check back with him in about a year or so.

But the door closed behind him without Abby having gotten one word out. She set her glass down beside his, picked up a soft pillow and flung it at the door. She

just wished she knew the real reasons behind doing
that.

It took her forever to fall asleep that night, and the
next morning Abby awoke in no mood to wear violet
or any of the other more vibrant colors in her closet.
She snatched out her most somber black suit with the
high Victorian lace collar, and brushed her hair into a
sophisticated, but no-nonsense, French twist.

When she arrived at the courthouse, Delores was already at her desk. She took one look at Abby and
asked if she'd missed an important obituary notice in
the morning papers.

"Very funny," Abby muttered. "Whose side are you
on, anyway?"

Aaron came in shortly afterward and Abby was annoyed that he looked as though he'd slept like a baby.
Though she poured him a cup of coffee, as usual, she
told herself it was not a gesture, but rather because she
had finally accepted that it wasn't her concern whether
he was ingesting too much caffeine or not.

"Thanks," he said, taking a sip. "I like that blouse."

"It's not new."

"Maybe not, but it makes your neck look delectable."

She beat a hasty retreat back to her office before he
could catch her blushing.

Things got progressively more difficult after that. At
every opportunity, he said something personal, and
even when they weren't alone, he made a point to touch
her shoulder, place a hand at the small of her back or
stroke his thumb across the nape of her neck. It got to

where she was constantly looking over her shoulder for
fear of being caught off guard. She did not want him
to see the effect his attentiveness was having on her. At
the same time, a part of her worried that it was all a
fleeting dream. Had she been wrong about him? Could
he really care?

She was in the supply room down the hall, using the
copier machine when he wandered in and shut the door
behind himself. The moment Abby heard the faint click
of the lock being set, her stomach began filling with
fluttering butterflies.

"You'd better not do that," she warned, almost
successful at keeping her voice brisk and free of tension. "You know how fast gossip spreads around
here."

"Do I look worried?"

No, he looked up to no good, as well as devastating
in his three-piece navy suit. Abby tore her gaze from
him and tried to remember if she'd already made a
photostat of the document on the machine's window or
had she been about to? Muttering under her breath, she
leaned over to check the exit tray.

After determining there was no copy, she straightened, to find Aaron beside her. Before she could react, he slipped his hand under her chin and lifted her
head for a brief but warm kiss.

"Thanks," he murmured, smiling into her eyes. "I
needed that."

"Aaron . . . you're crazy."

"What's the matter? You said you wanted romance. Isn't spontaneity part of that package?"

"*Not* during office hours," she ground out, clenching her hands into fists, in order to keep from clutching at his lapels and begging him to do it again.

"Fickle, fickle," he teased, stroking her cheek before dropping his hand. "I have a proposition for you."

"I'm busy, and if you want my notes on the Jacobson case before I leave, you'd better get out of here."

"This is for Saturday, not today." He rested an elbow on the lid of the machine, making it impossible for her to do anything but pay attention to him. "I've heard about an estate sale in Palm Beach. I thought we could go see what's available. The deceased was a staunch Democrat. Who knows? Maybe there'll be an elephant or two floating around."

Abby couldn't believe her ears. He actually wanted to do something like that? "Since when are you interested in estate sales?"

"Well, I'm not big on flea markets, but I'm trying to show you that when I'm inspired—" He took one of her hands and, uncurling her fingers, lifted them to his lips. "—I am willing to compromise."

The caress was tender and seductive, and Abby almost forgot to answer. "I wouldn't want you to spend what free time you do have going someplace you couldn't care less about."

"Abby, dear..." He grasped her hand more firmly and placed it against his chest. "If it would interest *you*, it would interest me. How else am I going to find out about all that makes you tick? Say yes, and I'll throw in a lobster dinner. That's my top offer. Oh, what the heck, I'll throw in a bottle of champagne, too."

Feeling more like a teenager than a mature woman, Abby laughed. Dear heaven, she wanted to accept. Should she take the risk?

She nodded. "All right. I'd love to go."

Chapter Nine

The auction was by invitation only, and while Abby didn't question Aaron's social clout in obtaining one of the engraved cards assuring them entry, she wondered at the phone calls he must have made to achieve it. The Delmont estate was spread over two acres of breath-taking landscape; a golf-course-perfect lawn, towering palm trees and shrubbery that looked more lovingly tended than the hairdos on some of the dowagers who were ascending the front stairway. Wrought-iron fencing encompassed the entire property and security guards were placed at the front gates, the front door and throughout the house and property.

The mansion itself was straight out of either Hollywood or a fairy tale, Abby couldn't decide which. Two-storied and built in a wide U, its brick walls had been painted a noxious pink. Abby whispered to Aaron that now she knew what had caused the owner to expire.

Inside, the contradictions multiplied. While the house, itself, was architecturally impressive—in the foyer alone, the floor was made of imported marble from Italy and the wood for the paneling had been imported from the already dwindling forests of Malaysia—whoever had added the finishing touches to the place had more of an affection for flash than refinement.

"I guarantee we'll find you an elephant here," Aaron murmured behind his program, as they followed the crowd to the first display room. "No doubt a few plastic flamingos, as well."

Abby shot him a discreet poke in his ribs, but grinned. But he was right; one had to pay attention to find the treasures in between the trash. As Aaron went off to get them both a glass of complimentary champagne, Abby wandered through what had apparently been a ballroom. Along the way, she saw that an exquisite Chinese urn was placed beside three wooden masks from Thailand—interesting, to be sure, but hardly of comparable provenance. Some time after that, she noted a Remington lithograph next to an autographed photo of a TV idol with his arm around a platinum blonde. Abby leaned closer to read the inscription. "To Roxie, the best limbo partner ever," she murmured.

"The bereaved widow," Aaron intoned, when she straightened.

She'd been wondering what happened to him. She was halfway through this part of the display. "How did you glean that bit of information?" she asked, accepting the fluted glass of champagne he offered her.

"I ran into her back in the foyer."

"Why am I not surprised?" Abby eyed the photo with more amusement than before. The woman's eyelashes were almost as thick as they were long; it made her feel better.

"Be nice. The only reason I lingered to introduce myself was because of you."

"Really? I can't wait to hear how you intend to make that line sound even remotely credible." Just then, she heard a tinkling laugh rise over the hum of conversation around the room. Glancing toward it's source, she spotted the "bereaved widow" herself, resplendent in a silk gown that looked more appropriate for a boudoir than an auction. When the wind-chime laughter erupted again, Abby averted her gaze to study the bubbles rising to the top of her glass. "May you turn to salt, if you're the slightest bit tempted to look over your shoulder."

"Don't you know I only have eyes for you? Anyway, you'll regret saying that, when I give you the scoop on a certain treasure she told me about. Come with me to the jewelry display," he said, taking hold of her elbow and steering her toward the last aisle by the floor-to-ceiling windows.

Abby was having fun. After worrying herself to a state for the rest of the week, she was now glad she'd accepted his invitation. And didn't he look sporty in his navy blazer and gray slacks? She was glad she had chosen to wear her newest summer dress, a strapless sheath in camel with a white bolero jacket.

It took Abby a moment to realize the last aisle consisted of display cases of small items such as pens, perfume bottles and assorted knickknacks, as well as jewelry. "In case you haven't noticed before, I'm not into jewelry," she murmured to Aaron. She rarely wore more than a watch, a necessity in her job, and earrings. She hadn't even worn a ring, since taking off the diamond Brad had given her.

"It won't hurt to look," Aaron insisted, scanning the contents in the glass cases while guiding her. "Ah! There it is."

Following his pointed finger, Abby looked down to see the gold-and-jade bracelet. It was delicately made and obviously expensive. It was also far too—ornamental for her taste, that was even if she liked bracelets. But then she realized all the jade charms dangling from it were elephants.

"Oh..."

"I told you so. She said Snookums—don't look at me like that, I swear that's what she said he liked her to call him—picked it up for her when they went to Shanghai to celebrate their third wedding anniversary. She's going to miss him terribly."

"I'm sure. No wonder she's liquidating everything but his sock garters."

"IRS problems. That's what finished off Snookums. He heard he was in for a full audit and went out like a light. Roxie'll be lucky if she's left with five or six million."

"An American tragedy." Abby leaned closer to the case to better appreciate the detailed carving on the jade. It really was lovely, she mused. "It'll probably go for a small fortune."

"It probably would have, if the lady wasn't prone to sentimentality and gestures. It's already sold," Aaron explained at Abby's confused glance.

Indeed, no sooner did he speak, than a man walked over to the one standing guard over the case. After whispering something to him, the second man drew out a key, unlocked the case and removed the bracelet.

"No! But that's not legal, is it? Where can I file a protest?" As the piece of jewelry was placed into a box and carried away, Abby scoped the room for someone who looked stuffy and authoritative enough to be overseeing this whole production.

Aaron tugged her back. "What a little Hun you are," he chuckled with delight. "Drink your champagne and calm down."

"But I want a chance at that bracelet."

"You don't need one. It's yours. I'm the one who bought it."

She stared at him, as though he'd just told her he had bought Rockefeller Center from the Japanese. Then with a hushed cry of joy, she threw her arms around him. "Aaron! Really? Oh, my goodness."

"Watch the champagne, sweetheart. We're too far from Miami for me to drive home and change clothes, okay?"

"Oops—sorry." Still, Abby could barely contain her elation. "This is wonderful. I don't know what to say."

In response, Aaron touched his glass to hers. "Just say that you're having a good time and that you're not sorry you came."

She could do better than that and, not caring who was watching, she stepped closer and gave him a slow, intimate kiss. "I'm very happy I came," she whispered, gazing into his eyes. "Thank you."

When they parted, Aaron's eyes were positively glassy and her knees felt weak.

"Is it too early to make a polite exit?" he asked thickly.

"I've got news for you, it's too early for this champagne," Abby laughed. "Let's go see what else we can find." Looping her arm through his, she led him to the next room.

The moon resembled a melon-ball scoop on a backdrop of sapphire satin when Aaron finally pulled his sedan in front of Abby's apartment. He helped her collect the treasures she'd accumulated during their day together, the silver-thread-and-teal-satin floor pillows the Delmonts had acquired during a trip to the Middle East, the crystal night-table lamp and a gaudy brass bull door knocker that he still couldn't understand her bidding on.

"You have a door knocker," he noted, as she unlocked the front door and turned on a black-shaded side-table lamp.

"True." Abby carried the flowers he'd bought her from a roadside vendor to the kitchen. "But it's not for me, it's a gift for Delores's Marty."

"Ah. Lucky soul."

"You'd have to know the full story about Marty and bulls to appreciate the humor."

Aaron dropped the pillows near the coffee table and was surprised to see how the flashiness of the silver threading was toned down in Abby's more conservative environment. With a wry shake of his head, he then set the lamp on the console TV. She could decide where she wanted it herself, he decided and slumped down on the couch, pleasantly tired.

"Can I get you a cup of coffee? A brandy?" Abby asked, returning with the vase and flowers. Setting them on the coffee table, she eyed him questioningly.

She made him ache, standing there in the soft lamplight. The day had turned out to be a scorcher, and she had removed her jacket on the ride home, as he had. The muted light shimmering on her shoulders also turned her hair into a halo of gold that had his stomach tightening with desire. "I'd rather have you come here."

He extended his hand, and though it took only seconds before she gave him hers, it seemed more like forever. Was this what it felt like to fall in love? he wondered, drawing her down beside him on the couch. It must. All day long, the emotions had been coming at him like a slow-moving front. Whatever he did, whenever he spoke, he had one eye, one ear tuned in to Abby, as if she were an entirely new person he was getting to meet.

He was in love with her. Of course, it hadn't just happened today, but had been developing...well, naturally. For years she had been his employee, confidant, friend, and very often the bane of his existence, he thought, with a wry smile. But somehow she had also become more. She had crept her way inside his heart, so deep he knew he would never get her out. He didn't even want to think of trying.

"What are you smiling at?"

"You," he replied, drawing her closer so that she was half reclining against his chest. "I've decided I like looking at you."

"You're getting to be an awfully easy man to please."

"That's what you think." He let himself be hypnotized by her eyes, let his need build. "You know what would be a perfect ending to this day?"

"Don't say anything edible, because not only haven't I been to a grocery store this week, but I'm so full I'm about to burst."

"No woman who passed up a lobster for a salad can be full."

"Don't tease. I hate the way they cook them, Aaron. It's cruel."

"But delicious."

"If I'm a Hun, as you said, then you're a hedonist."

Maybe. She certainly tempted him to show her how bad he could be. Instead, however, he focused on showing her how special she was to him. "For someone who was so poor as a kid, it's amazing that you can pass up on so much of the good life," he said stroking her back.

"No, it's not. I just don't need a lot of flashy things and expensive foods to make me happy. Tell me one instance where a good lobster dinner saved the world? Cured a major illness? Cleaned up politics?"

"Now you sound like a proper minister's daughter. Had he lived, your father would have been proud of the way you turned out."

"No." Abby rested her cheek against his chest. "My divorce would have devastated him. He wouldn't have liked Brad, in the first place, but he definitely wouldn't have approved of my walking out on him. It was hard enough on Momma."

Aaron had never met either of Abby's parents, though her mother had died shortly after her daughter's separation. He forced himself to turn his thoughts on her ex-husband, the greatest source of the unhappiness in her life. It still amazed him that the man had shown no remorse over his infidelities or his behavior toward her. To think she had once accused *him* of being a user like her ex. "Do you still think of Brad sometimes?"

"He makes it hard to ignore him. He's on TV so much and in the newspaper. It helps that I usually skip the sports section and rarely watch TV except for the news. Why?"

He shifted a hand to her chin and coaxed her head up so she could meet his gaze. "Because I'm a selfish man, and when I kiss you I want to know you're going to think only of me."

He could feel her breath catch, her breasts respond, tighten. "Why don't you try it and find out?" she whispered.

She touched her lips to his. The honesty and sweetness of the gesture pierced him, locking his breath in his throat. And then it was all sensation, and the rightness of it was a balm.

Yes, this was what he wanted, had wanted seemingly for forever. He slid his hands into her hair and moved his mouth over hers, tasting, brushing, nipping. A soft moan rose from deep in her throat, and it made him think of all the other sounds he would like to draw from her. His vivid imagination kicked his temperature skyward.

"I've wanted to do this all day," he murmured, running his lips across her cheekbone, down her jawline. "Be alone with you."

"Me, too."

"On the way home, I wanted to pull onto a remote section of beach and just—hold you."

"I'll bet," she drawled.

He could hear her uncertainty war with hope and it made him feel all the more tender toward her. "Well," he allowed, "I suppose we would have thought of one or two other things to do."

The jade elephants dangling from her bracelet clicked together like a series of tiny castanets, as she ran her hand over the taut muscles of his shoulders and chest. "I'm sure. But it was so early. You would have gotten us arrested."

"That's what I figured." He brushed his lips against her smooth forehead. "This is nicer."

"Aaron...?"

"Hmm?"

"Stop talking and kiss me again."

Oh, yes. Again and again. He took her mouth more possessively this time and before he was through, they had shifted position and she was lying back on the couch, her hair fanning out making her look seductive and glorious.

"God, you feel good," he said feeling his own body grow hard as it reveled in the feel of her feminine curves. He let his gaze wander downward over the bare expanse of creamy skin to the gentle rise of her breasts. Without a word he lowered his head and ran his lips along the line where dress began and skin ended. "I can feel your heart pounding." He glanced up at her. "You're not uncomfortable with this, are you?"

"Why should I be?"

"Because I want more."

And to show her how much, he slid his hand beneath her and, holding her gaze with his, he lowered her zipper. Then he brushed the dress's bodice downward with his chin. As he had guessed, she wore no bra. She didn't need to, he thought closing his mouth over her left breast.

Abby arched off the couch, her fingers biting into his shoulders. "Aaron..."

"I'll stop whenever you want." But not yet, he hoped in silence, shifting to award the same caress to her other breast. She was perfect, and her rosy nipples were soon rigid with a need that was reinforced by the subtle shifting of her hips against his.

Heaven help him, he wanted her. He'd never wanted a woman in quite this way before. His body throbbed with it and his heart yearned. Would it be moving too fast? Granted, he could tell she wanted him, too, and they certainly weren't children. But...this was, after all, only their first real date. What kind of message would he be giving her if he asked for this ultimate gift, after only spending barely one day together?

No, she'd been right when she'd spoken about being used and feeling cheated. First, he needed to prove she meant more to him than a sexual release.

With a last longing gaze, he hid her delectable body from his view and rezipped her dress. "You have to do us both a favor and throw me out of here," he grumbled, not quite able to be a good sport about it.

"It's not that late."

With a wry smile, he drew her up and off the couch. "It's later than you think." But unable to deny himself entirely, he folded her close and stole one last kiss.

Well, stealing wasn't exactly the correct term, he amended, when he finally ended it to get his bearings. Abby was too sweet, too generous for their mutual good. He pressed her head against his shoulder and fought to resist the urges his body was bombarding him with.

"What are your plans for tomorrow?" he asked, his voice dry and raspy to his own ears.

"I—um, I don't know. Clean house, do the wash or something."

"What a waste for a Sunday. Let's have brunch at one of the downtown hotels, and argue over what movie to see afterward."

"You once said you don't like movie theaters because of the noisy audiences and the surprises you invariably find on the floors."

True, but it was less dangerous than renting videos and staying here or at his place. About to confess as much to her, he remembered what date tomorrow was. "There's going to be a new concert opening for the outdoor musical series in the park near my place. It's Broadway shows, this time around, and I have season tickets. What do you say?"

"Why yes, of course."

* * *

She said "yes" again and again in the days that followed. They went to plays, to dinners that ranged from the exotic to homey, and to concerts. In addition, as a result of their houseboat adventure, Aaron had decided he was finally ready to buy a boat to tie up at his private dock, and so they also spent considerable time going from marina to marina viewing the offerings. Abby's favorite days, however, were those then they simply went for a drive to view the ever receding marshlands or took a long walk in a park.

The days slid into weeks and before she knew it, it was September. When Abby thought back on the summer, she couldn't believe it had passed this quickly. On the other hand, though, happy as she undoubtedly was, there were shadows of doubt diminishing her joy, because Aaron seemed content to take their relationship only so far and no further.

She had to be crazy. Most women would worry that a man was pushing to get into bed with them, yet here she was putting herself into a state by wondering why Aaron hadn't suggested they take their relationship to the next step. She wasn't a prude, nor was she Victorian in her beliefs; if a woman loved a man, she believed in the rightness to exhibit that love in whatever way she deemed appropriate. She loved Aaron, and she wanted to make love with him. What was the problem?

Several times during the past few days, she had given him subtle hints; in this day and age, she saw no reason why a woman couldn't be the one to initiate lovemaking. But each time—though he seemed eager and

tempted—Aaron had stopped things before they had
gone too far. Abby didn't understand it. What else
could she do, short of telling him she loved him?
Surely, he had to know.

But what if he was having reservations about how far
he wanted their relationship to go? Or worse yet, what
if he'd changed his mind about her? That idea filled
Abby with dread and pain, and she quickly dismissed
the notion as ridiculous. But as one day slipped into the
next, the doubts came back to haunt her again and
again with increasing frequency.

They struck again on the first Tuesday after Labor
Day. Aaron had come in preoccupied, even distant.
They had had an exhilarating weekend that had cul-
minated the day before with their attending an evening outdoor concert and fireworks display. When
they'd arrived at her apartment, Aaron had accepted
her invitation to come inside and just as she had expected, *hoped* from the intimate looks he had been
sending her way all evening, she'd soon found herself
in his arms.

He had never been more amorous or frank about his
desire for her. But just when she'd anticipated he would
suggest they move to her bedroom, he withdrew and
instead reminded her that they both needed to get up
early in the morning. She should have asked for an explanation, but, once again, old worries stopped her.

"Would you believe I actually got downstairs in time
to grab the last two chocolate croissants?" Delores
said, upon entering her office.

Abby who had been slumped in her chair and swiv-
eling back and forth as she pondered her problems, sat

up abruptly and tried to sound at least mildly grateful. "Wonderful. I didn't feel like eating breakfast this morning and I could use something."

The truth was that she'd believed she was going to have breakfast with Aaron—they'd actually made a date for him to pick her up—only it had not happened. When he failed to show, she had phoned his house, thinking he'd overslept. There hadn't been any answer, so she'd come in to work on her own. When he finally arrived, minutes before he was due in court, his excuse had been that "something had come up."

"Hello? Abby, wake up!"

Abby gave herself a mental shake, and saw that Delores was leaning back from the utility area and trying to get her attention. "Excuse me, what did you say?"

Delores rolled her eyes. "I asked if you wanted your croissant heated in the microwave for a few seconds and whether you wanted coffee or tea?"

"Yes to the heating and coffee, please." If she was so out of it that she didn't hear her co-worker when she was only feet away from her, she needed all the stimulation she could get.

She busied herself by putting aside the university fund-raiser speech she'd promised to review and perhaps polish for Aaron, making room for her and Delores to take their break together. It came as no surprise to realize that while she knew she had already scanned the first page twice, she couldn't remember a word she'd read.

"Make way for this stuff." Aaron's secretary set down the paper plates containing their treats on Abby's desk. "My feet are killing me," she groaned, distributing the mugs she carried in her other hand. "Marty decided the perfect way to officially end the summer would be to attend the amateur golf tournament at the county country club. I must've walked ten miles, and I think my scalp's sunburned, too. What we do in the name of love. Did you and Judge M. do anything special?"

"We went to the concert and had a picnic dinner."

"Isn't that romantic? I told Marty it would be something like that." She took a bite of her croissant and shut her eyes. "Mmm...heaven, and I'm not going to think twice about these calories. What are you waiting for? Eat."

Though the croissant smelled wonderful and looked delicious, Abby's appetite had vanished at the mention of Aaron. She pushed the plate away and picked up her mug instead. "Maybe I'm coming down with a virus or something."

"There's one going around." Then older woman's eyes went wide. "Say, your aren't—you know what?"

"What?" Abby said, a little slow on following, because her thoughts kept drifting to her troubles. But when she finally caught on, she could feel heat burn in her cheeks. "No, of course not! How could you think that?"

"How could I not? You two have been practically inseparable, ever since you cleared up that misunderstanding. What else am I supposed to think? And, anyway, what's wrong with thinking it?"

"Because we aren't...we aren't...you know," Abby muttered, looking everywhere and anywhere to avoid Delores's all-too-shrewd gaze.

"Yeah, right," her friend scoffed. "And the pope is coming to my house for dinner on Sunday. Abby, this is me you're talking to. I've seen the way you look at him, the way he looks at you. What do you mean you 'aren't...?' What's the matter with you?"

"It's not *me*."

"Oh." Delores frowned, took another bite of croissant and chewed hard. "Makes no sense," she said at last.

"At least we agree on something. And I'm beginning to worry, too."

"Honey, you need to be more than worried. At this stage you need to have an all-out stress attack."

"Thanks so much. I can't tell you how much better you've made me feel." Abby put down her mug and buried her face in her hands, uttering a sound of despair. "I've tried to let him know how I feel. I've even tried to be mildly—assertive."

"Oh, I can just see you doing what Grace Kelly did to seduce Jimmy Stewart in *Rear Window*," Delores gushed, looking thoroughly enraptured.

"Well, I've got news for you, Grace was a lot more successful than I was."

"The bum."

"Delores, what's wrong with him? What's wrong with *me*?"

"I don't know, honey, but you better get him to sit down and talk it over soon. These things have a way of mushrooming, when you don't deal with them right from the beginning."

* * *

Abby knew Delores was right, but though she was willing to tackle her problem with Aaron head-on and as soon as possible, the opportunity wasn't forthcoming. By afternoon, she was of the distinct impression the man was trying to avoid her and it only added to her worries.

After he got out of court, he had a business luncheon with one of Miami's more high-powered attorneys, then a meeting with the mayor. Abby knew he'd been back in the office in between all this, but either she was off on an errand or he was with someone, making it impossible to speak to him about anything personal.

Determined to wait him out, no matter how long it took, she returned from the law library to find a message on her desk.

At first she was elated to see his masculine scrawl, but her happiness was soon obliterated when she read the message.

Have left for the day. Bring me the file on the Nolan case, as soon as you're ready with it. Drop it by the house on your way home.

A.

Abby slowly slumped down into her chair, feeling as though her very life's blood was seeping out of her. There was no "please," no "thank you," no message to let her know that he had missed her or was looking forward to seeing her later. In fact, the message looked very much as though he'd reverted back to his old behavior—a behavior she'd made it clear she abhorred and would never tolerate from anyone again.

"Oh, no," she whispered. "This can't be happening."

Chapter Ten

She counted on instinct alone to get her to Aaron's, because the rest of her was focused on what she was going to say once she got there. The material he had requested was beside her on the car's passenger seat. He would get what he'd asked for, all right—and a bit more.

Don't do anything foolish.

Was it foolish to feel as though you had been hit in the stomach with an iron fist? Was it foolish to love someone and ask only that they respect that love, or to live only for the day when they told you they loved you?

No more. She couldn't take these games, or whatever it was he was doing, any longer. She needed an explanation for this latest behavior; not that she was going to be able to give it merit. Only weeks ago, he had promised to try to never hurt her again. How long had that lasted?

Someone hit his horn behind her. Abby jerked back to consciousness and saw that the red light she'd been sitting through had already turned to green. Sucking in a deep breath, to ease the ache consuming her entire body, she shifted her foot from the brake to the accelerator.

There was no ignoring reality, she thought, as she turned into Aaron's estate moments later and offered a single nod to the security guard at the entryway. He obviously didn't want her. Maybe this was his way of trying to tell her that he had changed his mind; because he had cared at some point, she was certain of it. Unfortunately, there was no easy way to accept bad news when you loved someone the way she loved Aaron. If that was indeed the case, if he wanted to end their relationship, a part of her was going to die.

So you'll quit and start a new life elsewhere. Life goes on.

Yes, she thought swallowing at the lump that kept rising to her throat, but it still hurt. This was unlike any pain she had ever experienced.

She pulled into Aaron's driveway, shut off the engine and took another deep breath. Courage, she instructed herself. She'd gone through losing both her parents at a relatively young age, a miscarriage and a media-covered divorce. *This, too, shall pass.* Her purse and the Nolan file in hand, she climbed out of the car.

How many times had she walked up this sidewalk, admired this well-tended yard, the quiet elegance of his home? Would this be the last time? Abby bit her lip, then realized she hadn't even looked in the mirror to check if she had any lipstick left. She was wearing a new red coatdress today, and knew her face looked washed out without at least a dash of color on her mouth.

Give it a rest, Gordon.

The door swung open, before she could press the bell. "You're early," Aaron said, looking slightly harried, but still appearing ready to be photographed for a men's fashion magazine.

It was on Abby's tongue to come back with something about tolling bells and settling for what you get; but she got too caught up in the man himself to let the actual words out. He looked so wonderful; he had taken off his suit jacket and now wore his blue-striped shirt, navy slacks with the red suspenders she thought so stylish and sexy on him, along with the blue-and-silver tie she'd given him for his last birthday. The long-stemmed pink rose he was holding, however, disrupted the whole picture.

Looking from it to him, she shook her head. "Early?"

He followed her glance and laughed in embarrassment. "Have you any idea how difficult it is to get pink long-stemmed roses around here? Red's a cinch of course, but *pink*... Here." He offered it to her. "It'll look a whole lot better with you than with me."

Numb, Abby didn't know what else to do but accept it. It really was lovely, perfect. She bowed her head and lifted the bud to her nose to draw in its subtle scent, but also to hide, because her eyes were flooding.

"Don't just stand there, come on in. Give me these," he added, closing the door behind her and removing her purse and the file from her other hand and setting them on the entry table. "I've got to get back into the kitchen and check the duck. I cheated on the orange sauce, I hope you don't mind. It's from a jar, because I didn't want to risk creating a disaster."

He drew her along through the living room. Abby's high heels sunk deep in the pile rug and she almost stumbled. "Aaron..."

"Sorry, I didn't mean to drag you. I guess I'm more nervous and excited than I thought."

What was he nervous about? "We have to—"

"I've been working on getting this set up most of the day. Well, I actually started last night."

"You don't seem to realize—"

"Damn, I haven't even said hello properly, have I?"

Before she could get another word out, he kissed her. In some corner of her mind, Abby told herself to pull away, to stop him. But her heart was so greedy for this, she absorbed everything, anything he would give her.

When he finally lifted his head, Aaron absently touched his cheek and then stared at hers. "Oh, hell...I really blew it, didn't I? The note was too brisk. But don't you see? All I was trying to do was to make sure I'd get you over here. I didn't mean to hurt you again."

"Well, you've succeeded in doing both," she muttered, wiping at the trail of wetness coursing down both cheeks.

"The idea was to surprise you, but everything's going wrong. I don't even have all the roses in water, yet."

"Do you know how it felt to read your note ordering me, *ordering* me to—"

"I should have known it was going to backfire, from the beginning. I didn't get out of court as early as I'd hoped. They were late in delivering the flowers. The duck didn't defrost as quickly as I'd thought it would." He framed her face with his hands. "And I've made you cry. Abby, sweetheart, this was all a ruse."

"All I realize is that one of us is crazy and the other is completely confused," she muttered, torn between wanting to punch him, for scaring the wits out of her, and slowly coming to the realization of the meaning behind all this.

"How else could I guarantee getting you here, except by making it a command appearance?"

"Did it ever cross your mind to just invite me to dinner?"

He shrugged, his eyes taking on a mischievous glint. "That would have been too simple. Boring. Besides, it would show my hand," he added, reaching into his pocket. "You see, my motive wasn't only to feed you dinner."

He uncurled his fingers exposing a small black-velvet-and-gold box. Abby's heart stopped. She stared in growing wonder as he opened it to display a single impressive diamond, flashing pink and blue and gold against white satin.

"This was supposed to be dessert, my grand finale," he murmured wryly. "But I can see that you're in dire need of some reassuring." Slipping the ring out of its slot, he tossed the box on a nearby chair and took Abby's left hand, which had been clenched around the rose. Holding the ring at the tip of her fourth finger, he lifted his gaze to hers. "Abigail Gordon, will you do me the honor of becoming my wife?"

She couldn't speak, but afraid the dream would shatter and she would wake up if she didn't reply, Abby nodded vaguely and then again with more certainty. Exhaling his relief, Aaron slid the ring the rest of the way onto her finger. It fit as though made for her, and beginning to believe in miracles, Abby decided it might have been.

"I don't know what to say," she whispered.

He laughed softly and drew her hand into his arms. "I'll coach you. First you tell me, 'It's lovely, Aaron.'"

"It's the most beautiful thing I've ever seen."

"Even better." He rewarded her with a tender kiss. "Then you say, 'This is such a surprise.'"

"You know it was. I was ready to beat you with that file," she admitted. "After which I was planning to walk out of here and promise myself never to see you again."

He winced, but then planted two kisses on either side of her lips. "In that case, we'll skip the rest of the ego stroking and get to the good part." He tilted her head back, forcing her to meet his emotion-filled eyes. "Finally, you tell me that you love me as much as I love you."

"Oh . . . I do, Aaron. I love you so much it hurts."

"Darling."

This kiss she would remember for the rest of her life. This kiss came with nothing held back, and it was full of promises and unrestrained desire. Her heart overflowing with joy, Abby responded with equal honesty, until they were both shaking and breathless.

"Ah, Abby... Abby. It feels good to say it. I love you."

"I love you."

"Surprised?"

"Blown away. I thought you were a hopeless case."

"Not to mention a few other things, eh?" he added with a dry laugh. Aaron shook his head. "I'm sorry for putting you through this, sweetheart, and for the long wait. I just wanted you to have time, to be sure."

"You can't be serious? I've been a lost cause about you forever."

Bemused, he arched his left eyebrow. "You've alluded to that before. Exactly how long?"

"I think I started falling in love with you the night you stayed with me after my accident."

"My God. You hid it so well." He stared at her with wonder. "You sneak. And here I thought I was losing my mind, whenever I started having covetous thoughts about you."

"Really? When did you know?"

"I was a bit slower," he admitted, "but something kicked in about the time we were planning our trip. Your reaction to me when I kissed your finger that day."

"You didn't kiss it, you—"

"Yes, I did, and I'll do it again," he murmured against her lips. "And lots more. I can't wait."

Their next kiss was slow and languid and ever so much more sensual than Abby could have dreamed.

This kiss had them pressed together, yearning and uttering sighs of pleasure.

"Abby, I want you so much."

"And I thought it was the duck that was beginning to burn."

Sniffing, Aaron muttered an oath and, pulling her along with him, hurried to the kitchen. He released her only long enough to take the duck out of the oven and put it on top of the stove. Then he drew her close again.

"See what you do to me?"

"It only looks a little well-done. The way I feel, I would rave about it if it was charred. Why don't you finish what you need to in here and I'll get the rest of these roses in water?" Abby suggested, stroking his cheek with the bud she still held.

"How can you be so practical at a time like this?" he complained, though his tone was teasing. "Here I am ready to sweep you off for my grand seduction scene and you're trying to make me focus on the mundane."

Abby felt a fleeting wave of shyness. "I was trying not to appear too eager."

The sound that emerged from Aaron's throat was not unlike a big cat's purr. "That's more like it," he murmured, seeking her lips yet again. Heat merged with heat, as silent questions were asked and answered. "Are you sure I'm not rushing you, love? Have I succeeded in bringing you at least a little of the romance you deserve?"

"The rest of our lives will be a romance," Abby replied, knowing in her heart that was the truth.

As Aaron opened his mouth to respond to that, the phone rang. "Damn," he muttered to the ceiling. "I forgot to turn on the machine. Let's take it in the living room."

He led her to the camel leather couch and drew her down beside him before snatching up the receiver. He'd barely said hello, when his face transformed into a wide grin. "Hey," he greeted, adding aside to Abby, "It's the girls."

She listened as he chatted with them, hearing snatches of the conversation because he held the phone where she could listen, and the girls—all three on extensions—kept getting progressively more excited and louder. They had just gotten home from their first day back at school and they'd wanted to share everything with him. Abby was so pleased for all of them. It appeared that Sean and Betsy's marriage was back on a solid foundation, and now he and the girls were deepening their relationship.

After they were through with their stories, Aaron told them about the engagement, and had to temporarily hold the receiver at arm's length because of all the screeches and shouts of glee.

"Can we come to the wedding?"

"I wanna be *in* it."

"Am I too old to be a flower girl?"

Aaron played with Abby's fingers, as he tried to answer question after question. It was soon apparent, however, that there wasn't going to be an end to the volley. Abby decided it was her turn and relieved him of the phone.

She told the girls that they hadn't yet made any definite plans, but that she thought it would be wonderful if they could come down and be her attendants.

THREE LITTLE CHAPERONES   189

After promising them they could have some input on the colors of their dresses, she handed the phone back to Aaron.

"Okay," Aaron said, interrupting the new surge of chatter. "We're going to cut this short, but we'll talk to you and your parents within the next day or two, all right? Yes, Mitch, you can say one more thing."

When he finally hung up, Aaron groaned. "Yikes. I think I'm deaf in this ear."

"It's so sweet that they wanted to share their first schoolday with you," Abby murmured, resting her head on his shoulder. "We'll have to find out when they have a vacation break and schedule the wedding around it."

"That's not all."

"What do you mean?"

"Are you ready for this? Mitch said they decided they'd had such a good time down here that they want to come back next summer and stay with us while their parents take another vacation."

Abby couldn't help but laugh at his bewildered expression. "Don't worry," she assured him, snuggling closer. "We'll manage."

"Are you sure?" he drawled, shifting her onto his lap.

Abby nodded and slipped her arms around his neck. "Positive. Together we can handle anything."

And reaching back to take the phone off the hook, she proved it to him.

* * * * *

SILHOUETTE® Desire™

SILHOUETTE Desire 10TH Anniversary COLLECTION

Silhouette Desire 10th Anniversary

Celebrate with a FREE classic collection of romance!

In honor of its 10th Anniversary, Silhouette Desire has a gift for you! A limited-edition, hardcover anthology of three early Silhouette Desire titles, written by three of your favorite authors.

Diana Palmer   SEPTEMBER MORNING
Jennifer Greene   BODY AND SOUL
Lass Small   TO MEET AGAIN

This unique collection will not be sold in retail stores and is only available through this exclusive offer. Look for details in Silhouette Desire titles available in retail stores in June, July and August.

SDANN

H.R.
good

FREE GIFT OFFER

To receive your free gift, send us the specified number of proofs-of-purchase from any specially marked Free Gift Offer Harlequin or Silhouette book with the Free Gift Certificate properly completed, plus a check or money order (do not send cash) to cover postage and handling payable to Harlequin/Silhouette Free Gift Promotion Offer. We will send you the specified gift.

FREE GIFT CERTIFICATE

ITEM	A. GOLD TONE EARRINGS	B. GOLD TONE BRACELET	C. GOLD TONE NECKLACE
# of proofs-of-purchase required	3	6	9
Postage and Handling	$1.75	$2.25	$2.75
Check one	☐	☐	☑

Name: _____

Address: _____

City: _____ State: _____ Zip Code: _____

Mail this certificate, specified number of proofs-of-purchase and a check or money order for postage and handling to: HARLEQUIN/SILHOUETTE FREE GIFT OFFER 1992, P.O. Box 9057, Buffalo, NY 14269-9057. Requests must be received by July 31, 1992.

PLUS—Every time you submit a completed certificate with the correct number of proofs-of-purchase, you are automatically entered in our MILLION DOLLAR SWEEPSTAKES! No purchase or obligation necessary to enter. See below for alternate means of entry and how to obtain complete sweepstakes rules.

MILLION DOLLAR SWEEPSTAKES
NO PURCHASE OR OBLIGATION NECESSARY TO ENTER

To enter, hand-print (mechanical reproductions are not acceptable) your name and address on a 3"×5" card and mail to Million Dollar Sweepstakes 6097, c/o either P.O. Box 9056, Buffalo, NY 14269-9056 or P.O. Box 621, Fort Erie, Ontario L2A 5X3. Limit: one entry per envelope. Entries must be sent via 1st-class mail. For eligibility, entries must be received no later than March 31, 1994. No liability is assumed for printing errors, lost, late or misdirected entries.

Sweepstakes is open to persons 18 years of age or older. All applicable laws and regulations apply. Sweepstakes offer void wherever prohibited by law. Prizewinners will be determined no later than May 1994. Chances of winning are determined by the number of entries distributed and received. For a copy of the Official Rules governing this sweepstakes offer, send a self-addressed, stamped envelope (WA residents need not affix return postage) to: Million Dollar Sweepstakes Rules, P.O. Box 4733, Blair, NE 68009.

✂

SR1U

ONE PROOF-OF-PURCHASE
To collect your fabulous FREE GIFT you must include the necessary FREE GIFT proofs-of-purchase with a properly completed offer certificate.

(See center insert for details)